BATTLE S
from those \

"This book is a gut check for those who have worn the cloth of the nation. For those who have not, it is a testimonial for those who have served and sacrificed. As Americans we are blessed with freedom. It comes at a price."

-- James E. Livingston
Major General USMC (Ret)
Medal of Honor Recipient

"This book was a tough read, and at the same time I couldn't put it down. Salkin got this one right! Every now and again you come across a book that is as much cathartic as it is entertaining. At a time when we are losing way too many Soldiers, Sailors, Airmen and Marines, it struck a chord with this Old Soldier."

-- Colonel William L. Peace, Sr.
U.S. Army National Guard

"David Salkin has fired at close range and with unerring accuracy with this tale! He takes a tough situation that is all-too-often neglected and gives it life. This story is for all veterans and their supporters. His first-person writing style makes the reader feel present throughout the story. It's a quick read that will leave you thinking long after completion. I most strongly recommend it to all who are interested in understanding better the true costs of America's conflicts—past, present, and future. "

Major General GT Garrett, USA (Ret)
42nd Infantry Division

"David Salkin's story is a must-read for all Veterans and supporters. This book not only entertains you, it educates you on the price paid by those who have the guts to walk the walk. His first-person writing takes you on a ride which seems to bring out all emotions and it also places you right on the battlefield. Maybe it's just my love of heroic deeds but it sure knocked me on my knees. The read is overall life-like and is very consistent with the actions taking place every day in Iraq and Afghanistan. Kudos to Dave for really knocking this one out of the park."

Christian S. DiMeo (Ret) SFC.
USMC/Embassy Marine Cairo/Beirut/Geneva - ARMY NG/Operation
Enduring Freedom

"Battle Scars" hits like an RPG! Camaraderie, adrenalin, fear, loss, hope and redemption all in one exhilarating and disturbingly beautiful tale. Hard to believe David hasn't been on the battlefield, because this tale rocked me back for days! A must read for everyone who is, has been, or supports our warriors!"

-- Wayne Emery CPT, USA
Military Assistance Command Vietnam, I Corps
Team Leader, Advisory Team 1 and Advisory Team 3

"David Salkin is a masterful writer, I felt as if I was riding along in that up armored HUMVEE. Battle Scars is an incredible story of brothers in arms and the bonds formed in combat. The struggles that are faced by combat veterans returning from war are real and nothing I've read brings that story to life like Battle Scars. This is a must read!"

-- LTCOL T. Kevin White "TK" - USAF
150th Special Operations Wing

"Dave hit the nail on the head with this one. It's a quick read simply because you don't want to stop turning the page. This may be fiction but it certainly doesn't read that way."

"For anyone who's ever been there, this book brings back all the sights, sounds and smells of deployment like none other. Take care in the reading because Battle Scars is real. An often painful, always enthralling reminder of what we give...and what we lose...whenever we send our men and women to war. Mr. Salkin brought to life the pain and struggles of our fellow veterans and showed an accurate account of their bravery off the field."

"Our Marine, men and women, today are the best disciplined, committed and honorable warriors period. They are writing new chapters in the long honorable legacy of our United States Marine Corps. People this is simple! Combat Marines join the legacy of our Marine Corps with their commitment to victory in its missions, by our own sacrifice or by joining our fallen heroes. We are bound in honor to leave our nation's enemy defeated, broken, and destroyed. We never leave Marines behind, ever. This story reminds us all that today's challenges also take the same sacrifice and commitment that was rendered in the past by some to help us all."

Semper Fidelis,

For Marie —

Hope you like the story,
good luck with your writing!
Dave

DMSalkinAuthor @ gmail.com

Battle
Scars

David M. Salkin

ISBN-13: 978-1545141830

ISBN-10: 1545141835

BATTLE SCARS

Edited by Monique Happy Editorial Services

Cover art by Alexander von Ness

alexander@nessgrapics.com

Please visit Dave on Facebook (Author David M. Salkin), or follow Dave on Twitter @DavidMSalkin
Email: DMSalkinAuthor@gmail.com
Website: DavidMSalkin.com

AUTHOR'S NOTE

As of this writing, I've had thirteen novels published. It's always been with one goal in mind—to entertain my readers. Battle Scars is different. These pages were written to do more than entertain you. They were written to honor the men and women of the United States military and their families. There's a debt that can never be repaid, but at the very least, we can all say thank you. This is for them.

I've been privileged to work with many veterans over the years in various capacities. It's been an honor to be made "part of the family," including becoming an associate member of the Philip A. Reynolds Detachment of the Marine Corps League over ten years ago. I'm also a founding member of the Veterans Community Alliance – Freehold Township Day Committee, which helps local veterans and their families. We've given over a hundred thousand dollars to veterans in need over the past decade, and have made a positive impact for our New Jersey veterans and their families.

Over the past decade, veterans have shared personal stories with me, some of which I'll never forget. Some of the fictionalized anecdotal stories have been woven into Battle Scars. I'm sure these little anecdotes will jog memories for many veterans when they read this. Battle Scars is a journey. It's a story of courage, and pain, and hope. And I hope I've told this story in such a way that you, my readers, "get it." It's the only thing I've ever written that made me cry as I wrote it. Don't panic, it also made me laugh a few times. I just felt I needed to do more than twenty-two pushups. (The 22 Pushups a Day Challenge was a social media campaign to raise awareness of veteran suicides, in case you missed it.)

A portion of the profit from the sale of this book will go towards helping veterans through the veterans organizations with whom I work. For the veterans who have shared their personal stories with me over the years: Thank you. It's been such an honor and privilege to call many of you friends.

This book is dedicated to our veterans. Thank you for your service, and welcome home.

Chapter 1
Alive Again

I snapped awake like a mortar round going off. Screaming, I rolled across my tossed sheets, scrambling for a weapon that wasn't there. My hands searched through the bed covers on auto-pilot, even as I tried to convince myself I was safe in my own bed.

I'd woken up that same way a hundred times since my last day in Afghanistan, although sometimes the scream stayed stuck in my throat, making it hard to breathe. My heart was pounding so loudly I could hear it in my ears. I was sweating and terrified.

It was as much flashback as it was nightmare. The staff at Walter Reed had told me it would get better over time. "Post-Traumatic Stress Disorder," or PTSD; it was common after "incidents" like mine.

Incidents.

My incident happened twenty-one June, 2014 in a No-Name Shithole Village east of Kandahar. The incident almost killed me.

Our convoy was taking it slow along the dirt road that was "Main Street" through the village. We had started out of Patrol Base Boldak at oh-dark-thirty, so it was still early when we arrived at the village. It wasn't even supposed to be a part of the day's mission—we were heading much further east, or so we thought.

It was already eighty-five degrees and would be well over a hundred by noon. We were in a Humvee that none of us liked, and not just because of the crappy air conditioning. The same three guys that I was with that day had been with me in an up-armored version of this vehicle when we had hit an IED two months earlier. My gunny, Deke, used to say IEDs were like chicks. They came in three sizes: petite ones that would get your attention, medium-sized curvy girls that would throw you around pretty good, and the fat girls that might just kill you if they got ahold of you. *That* day, two months ago, we rolled over a petite girl. It lifted the truck off the ground a few inches, gave all of us a concussion and ringing ears for a few days, and had my best friend, Frank "Squid" Skidaro pissing blood for two days. Other than that, we ended up lucky. Light duty for ten days back at Camp Leatherneck, which suited all of us just fine, then back out to The Shit.

On *this* particular day, our Rhino, which is a heavy-weight up-armored transport vehicle, was out of service because of some damage it had taken a few days prior. We ended up with a version referred to as a POS, or *piece of shit*, in civilian terms. I was sitting in the rear right next to Johnny Mack. We were second vehicle from the front in a five-vehicle convoy. Squid was driving, and Chuck was riding shotgun. Because the air-conditioning in this particular POS kept the inside of our vehicle at about a hundred and thirty degrees, I cracked my door a bit and shoved my face out to the air outside.

Either Vehicle One missed the pressure plate, or the IED was detonated remotely, but as we rolled along at about fifteen miles an hour through the brown village, we hit a fat girl. An "EFP," or

Explosively Formed Projectile. For simplicity's sake, an IED that forms a copper slug capable of ripping even a tank apart.

I don't remember much of the explosion. Just the sensation of being weightless in a brilliant yellow light that was without sound. I ended up on the road about thirty feet from the smoldering wreck that had been the Humvee, lying on my back. At first, there was only bright light and silence. My ears weren't even ringing—just pure silence. No pain, no nothing. I was just lying there, weightless and in total peace. Everything was sort of gray.

And then things started to change very rapidly. The sound slowly came back on with a shrill ringing in my ears, and I could hear explosions and heavy gunfire. It was amazing to me, lying there flat on my back, how the world could go from such peaceful silence to the loudest noise level I'd ever heard. I tried to roll and find a weapon, but I couldn't move. I moved my head as best I could and watched as Marines scrambled everywhere, firing off magazines on full auto as RPG rounds screamed over me and exploded against our vehicles and the ground around us. Tracers danced over my face like the Fourth of July.

I knew we were in The Shit. I knew I was supposed to move and find cover. Problem was, I couldn't do a damn thing. I was telling my arms and legs to move, but they weren't cooperating. I started to feel nauseous and managed to roll my head to the side before I vomited. As I was spitting out the last of the nastiness, strings of it still attached to my bottom lip, my sergeant and best friend Deke slammed into me and started screaming at me. I watched his mouth moving and felt so calm. I couldn't hear anything he was saying—only gunfire and explosions. He lay across my chest and fired his weapon at someone I couldn't see. It's difficult to explain, but in all this noise, there was a sort of quiet. It's like it was so loud I couldn't hear anything, if *that* makes any sense. Deke's rifle didn't seem to make any noise at all. I could *feel* the recoil as his body moved against me each time he squeezed off a round, but I couldn't *hear* it. It was simply lost in the chaos around us.

After firing for a while, Deke took a knee next to me and grabbed my face. He was holding my face in his left hand, firing with his right, *screaming* at me, but I still couldn't hear anything. I watched his lips and thought he was saying, "You're gonna be all right," but I'm not sure. I saw him screaming again, this time not at me, and was pretty positive he was screaming "Doc!" He pulled a pressure bandage from his cargo pant pocket and I started thinking, *"That must be for me."*

Deke began firing again, and as I looked up at him kneeling over me, I could slowly start to feel my body again. It didn't feel good, either. A searing pain began to shoot up my legs and Deke looked down at me as I realized I was screaming. His face showed worry or fear or both, and *nothing* scared Deke. At that point, he started screaming back at me and stood up, grabbing me by my ILBE, or *Improved Load Bearing Equipment*, basically a vest full of straps and personal equipment. With his left hand on my left shoulder strap, and his right hand firing his weapon, he began dragging me out of the dirt road. My head and shoulders were now off the ground, and I could see, for the first time, what used to be my right leg.

At first, it was a surreal feeling, like I was looking at someone else's leg. There was a white bone below my right knee—my tibia, as I was later told, shining white and red in the hot sun. That was it. Nothing else. Just a white shiny bone where my right lower leg and foot were supposed to be. There was blood. Gallons of it, I think. I watched as the reddest blood I'd ever seen left a long red smear in the dry, baked dirt as Deke dragged me through gunfire that came in as thick as rain.

Deke dropped me behind what was left of a waist-high stone wall and began firing again. I think I was trying to talk to him. I think I asked him where my leg was. A corpsman dropped down next to me and started talking to me, but, like before, I could only see his lips moving. He placed a tourniquet around my knee and then popped a syringe into my other thigh. I didn't feel it, but I watched him do it with that same detached interest as when I'd seen my leg bone. I reached down with my right hand and squeezed my junk to make sure my man-parts were all still there. Thank God for that, at least.

The corpsman had to stop several times, covering my body with his own as rounds and explosions impacted all around us. The Muj[1] were definitely intent on killing all of us. At one point, I looked up and saw Deke standing, firing over the wall. The world began to go slow-motion, and I watched shell-casings pop out of Deke's rifle, still smoking, as he continued to fire at the enemy. His face was black with dirt, sweat running down in streaks, blood all over his hands and BDUs and face. Mine, I think. He looked like the most bad-ass human being I'd ever seen. His teeth were gritted together and he was talking to the enemy as he fired at them. As the world started to spin, I saw a puff of red mist around his left shoulder for a second, but after being knocked back for only

---

1 "Muj" – Mujahidin encompasses all Jihadist fighters in the Middle East. Terms of endearment used by American war fighters include The Muj, Hajis, and much more profane nicknames.

a second, he leaned forward and continued firing, now screaming at the enemy. And then again, "*puff.*" A little cloud of pink.

My last conscious thought at that time was looking up at Deke, who stood a hundred feet tall over me, and saying, "You *go*, boy …"

Deke.

Fuckin' Superman.

Chapter 2

2 June, 2014
Nineteen Days Before "The Incident"
Chuckie Spade

Johnny Mack was sitting on his ruck cleaning his M4, and Chuck was across on his own, reassembling his M240 Bravo, the squad's medium machine gun. "Chuck," Corporal Charles Adams, also referred to as "Spade" 'cause he'd put your ass in the ground, was a big motherfucker. The big dudes generally got stuck with the 240s because they were a bitch to carry, but Spade didn't complain. In fact, he loved that thing. A big boy with a big toy, we used to say. And let me tell you something, when the shit hit the fan and the Hajis were throwing lead at you, *no one* laid suppressing fire with such deadly accuracy as Chuckie Spade.

Spade tended to load his belts with more tracers than most guys. The problem with tracers is that they worked both ways, and your outgoing streaks of light were telling the bad guys where you were. Spade was so damn deadly with his shooting, he didn't give a shit. He hit almost everyone he ever shot at, and so they never had a chance to return fire. Deke told him to "chill on the sixes," meaning the M856 tracer rounds, and use more fives. The M855s were the regular rounds—but Spade never listened. Especially at night. I swear the big baby just liked watching the streaks of light send death to the enemy. In his defense, Spade always made sure he was away from everyone else, drawing fire to himself only. On more than one occasion, he'd put himself in harm's way while we outflanked the enemy, who was pinned down under Spade's withering fire.

Spade.

Fucking *animal*.

I loved that guy.

Chuckie Spade should have been an NFL star. He played college ball; had a full ride to Michigan as a defensive end until he tore his ACL and broke his leg. After he healed, his college football days were over, which meant so was his scholarship. To us, he was the greatest athlete we'd ever seen, but his speed wasn't what it used to be so his NFL shot was over. He dropped out of college and joined the Marine Corps, who was happy to have him, even with the less-than-perfect knee. He was a beast. Strongest guy in the platoon. But the best thing about having him with us was his parents.

Mom and Dad Spade sent care packages regularly. His dad was a blue-collar guy at a manufacturing plant in Chicago, and his mom worked at a grocery store. The standing joke was that she worked there just to keep enough food in the house for her husband and three boys, all of whom were huge. Not a month went by that we didn't get *something* from Mom Spade. She probably worked just to cover the food and shipping to us, and we loved her for it. On a few occasions when Spade could Skype home, we'd all be in the picture, eating their food from Chicago and singing "Thank you." There were a lot of shitty weeks when her packages helped us smile.

I smiled when I walked in and saw the two of them taking care of their weapons. "Glad to see you two fucktards are making sure your battle-rattle is shipshape."

Johnny Mack responded by holding up his M4 and smiling. "Yes, sir, General Nichols! My shit is wired tight and I am prepared to kill goat fuckers!"

"*Rah*, son!" I replied with a laugh. "And thanks for the promotion." It was nice to move from corporal to general so quickly.

"Where you been?" asked Mack.

"Took a run with the Squid," I replied.

Frank Skidaro was a lance corporal and our official platoon joker. The Squid was from New York City, and he joined the Corps as soon as he turned eighteen. His uncle had been a fireman, last seen running up the stairs of the North Tower when everyone else was running down. Squid joined for 9/11 payback, plain and simple. He earned a Bronze Star with a V for valor in his first month of his first deployment. A Bronze Star Medal can be awarded for exemplary conduct, or, in Squid's case, the Bronze Star Medal with a V device for valor, meaning the kid ran out of his hooch [2]with only his boxers, flip-flops, and weapon after finishing a shower just as the base came under attack.

The crazy bastard charged across the fire base under mortar attack, losing his flip-flops in the process, and killed three enemy

---

2 The United States Marine Corps speaks its own language, being born from the U.S. Navy. *Head* is the bathroom, *hooch* is your tent or sleeping quarters, *rack* is your bed, *Kevlar* is your helmet.

fighters wearing suicide vests who had managed to sneak to the wire in an attempt to breach the perimeter. Standing in the middle of the mortar barrage in his skivvies, Squid popped off three well-places rounds, one per Haji, taking down all three right at the perimeter. Haji Number Three detonated when Squid's round hit the man's vest, vaporizing the three Muj and knocking Squid about ten feet across the compound. By this time, the guards up in the tower had opened up with the heavy machine guns, and the attackers fled, seeing their suicide attack foiled by a skinny, half-naked, lunatic Marine.

Deke, our sergeant and squad leader, respected the kid's bravery as much as he worried about the kid's survivability. Squid was more balls than brains sometimes and occasionally needed babysitting. Deke had told him at least a dozen times he wasn't going to win the war by himself, but the little fucker was a crazy man when a fight started. His love for his uncle had turned into his hate for the enemy.

"How far?" asked Mack, referring to our run.

"Five klicks. It's hot as fuck outside, man."

"I don't know why you two are always running. We have *trucks*, you know."

I laughed. "The way our trucks run, it's good to be ready to run back to base."

"Yeah, no shit," mumbled Spade. "The Rhino still ain't back. We're going to get that POS Humvee again. I hate that thing."

"Can't Uncle Sam at least step up and get a Humvee with an AC unit that blows cold air? I think I sweated off five pounds last patrol," complained Mack.

"Where's Squid?" asked Spade.

"Head, shower, and hooch, then we're meeting for grub. You guys coming?"

"Hell yeah," said Chuckie Spade. "I heard rumors of decent pizza tonight."

Mack shook his head. "Oh, great. I can listen to you and Squid bitch about New York City versus Chicago pizza again."

Spade shrugged. "I *like* the deep dish pizza; fuck you guys."

"That ain't pizza, man," I said. "Squid's right. New York all the way. That shit was a bowl of doughy sauce."

"Amen. And the cheese goes on *top*, dude. What the actual fuck? Who puts the sauce on top of the cheese?" asked Mack.

Spade stood up. At six-five, two-seventy, he filled the hooch. "I'm eating my pizza. I'm going to *enjoy* my pizza. And I don't want to hear shit about it."

Mack and I exchanged glances. I wasn't gonna be the one to tell two-ton Spade his pizza sucked again. Never fuck with a man whose arms are bigger than your legs.

We headed out to the chow hall to see what today's surprise offerings would bring. I was praying for New York style pizza and not that bowl of shit Spade loved.

Chapter 3

2 June, 2014
Nineteen Days Before "The Incident"

Night Watch with Johnny Mack

Pizza night was the best thing that happened in a week. Pizza's like sex. Even shitty pizza is still pretty good. Definitely better than the MREs which made going to the bathroom a once-every-two-or-three-day event.

After pizza night, Johnny Mack and I had to take night watch in the south tower. It overlooked a million miles of countryside, and in another part of the world may have been a beautiful view. Not here. Not in the Muj sandbox. Everything was brown and baked and hid people who wanted to kill us.

We climbed up into the tower, built out of sandbags and metal and wood, and relieved the two tired Marines from Second Platoon. The .50 Cal Browning machine gun was mounted on a tripod, and in the hands of a United States Marine, it could rain death on the enemy with terrifying accuracy and violence from two thousand meters. Mack took a spot at the gun, and I sat next to him as spotter and loader.

We had a mounted night-vision binocular-type thing we called Big Eyes that was pretty amazing. I sat in a chair behind the thing, which looked like a weapon. It had two handles, just like the Browning, and a place to rest your chin as you looked into the box. It could be set for day- or night-vision, and you could see targets well out of range of our weapons. It was cool to use for the first five minutes—then just extremely boring, staring out to infinity, wanting to see someone you could shoot.

After a bit, I took my face out of the long-range binoculars and gave my eyes a rest. It was quiet, with most of our guys trying to grab some sleep.

Mack asked me, "Was Iraq like this?"

I thought about that for a second. "Yes and no. At least in Iraq you could work with some of the locals. And the Kurds were honorable people and good fighters we could depend on. If the Shias and Sunnis could ever stop massacring each other, they'd actually have a real country. Here in Ass-Crackistan? Shit. I ain't found one goat fucker I trust. Doesn't even feel like a country— just a bunch of Stone Age villages. I mean, the little kids in the villages, yeah, they're okay. But I guarantee you they'd blow your shit up in two seconds if the Muj told 'em to."

"Stress levels like this all the time?"

"Pretty much. Every time you'd relax a little, some guy would strap on a vest or drive his car into the gate. Fuckers are all crazy."

Mack got a little quieter. Almost embarrassed. "It's hard to sleep sometimes. I mean, even when things are quiet. I just can't ever relax, you know?"

"Yeah. Even when I got home from Iraq I couldn't sleep. It'll go away eventually. Don't do too many Rip Its and shit. Fucks with your brain."

"Tell that to Squid."

"He definitely needs to cut back."

Mack was quiet for a minute, then whispered, "Can I tell you something? I mean, you gotta promise not to say anything …"

"What's up?"

"I'm scared shitless like twenty-four-seven, man. I mean, when we go out on a mission I'm cool. I can function and do what I'm supposed to do. But when it gets quiet, I keep waiting for something bad to happen and I can't shake it, ya know? It's just like … I don't know …"

Mack took his hands off the gun and stared at them, checking to see if they were shaking.

"Listen, man, everyone here is scared shitless. You just got to tell yourself you're excited, not scared. When you get that feeling in your stomach, or you can't sleep—don't let it freak you out. Just say to yourself, 'I'm fired up!' *Convince* yourself you're excited, not scared. You'll be okay, man."

"You still get it sometimes?" he asked.

"Every fucking day, my man. Think of it as situational awareness. Keeps you on your toes." I took another long scan of the countryside.

"You think Deke still gets it?"

"Yeah. No. I don't know. He's a fuckin' warrior, dude. I think when you get to tour number three, it's just different. You're still wired up all the time, but you've accepted the situation, you know? You're just good with it. Whatever's gonna happen is gonna happen, and you know you'll be ready to do whatever needs to be done as long as you're still breathing."

I took my face out of the Big Eyes and smacked his arm. "Yo, man. Just relax a little. You're doing fine. Everyone's nervous on their first tour. When I think back on mine, I was more nervous that I'd fuck up and let my guys down than I was scared of the enemy, you know? But then the training kicks in when you're in The Shit, and you just go on autopilot, and it's all good. Take a huge deep breath, let it out, and just remember to keep breathing. I've watched you in The Shit—you're been a hundred percent, bro."

Mack let out a long sigh and said, "Thanks, man."

"Fuck it. Everybody looks out for each other. Don't sweat the Muj."

Neither of us spoke for a long time, lost in our own thoughts. I guess Mack's thoughts ended up back on me.

"You never talk about your family," he said.

"Not much to tell."

There was an awkward silence, and I knew he wanted to know more about the guy next to him. Our fire team was a little family, and we didn't hold back information from each other about anything. It was a fair question and time the new guy got his question answered.

"My family is the United States Marine Corps," I said quietly.

"Ooh Rah," he responded.

"No. Really. That's it. That's all I got. Just you fucktards. My dad split when I was really little, which I never understood because my mom was beautiful and sweet and everything a mom's

15

supposed to be. When I'd ask about him, she'd just change the subject and say we were all we needed—us two against the world. She made me feel invincible. Right when I turned eighteen, she got sick. Summer after high school. I was talking to her about college one minute and she was in the hospital the next."

"Shit," Mack whispered, the barrel of his machine gun sweeping back and forth for a quick scan.

"Yeah. Shit. I had decent grades, but we were kinda poor, I guess. I mean, I never thought much about it at the time. I was going to maybe go to community college for a couple of years and try and get a scholarship or something, you know? Mom was big on school. Wanted me to do something great out in the world. Next thing we know, we're in the hospital and she's got cancer everywhere."

"Oh, no."

"Man, it happened so fast. Mom had the longest, most beautiful brown hair. When I was really little I loved to sit on her lap and play with it. I was there when they shaved her head because it was coming out in clumps. Faked a big smile and told her how great she looked bald while I was dyin' inside. Three months of chemo and radiation and a surgery and she was dead anyway. Worst three months of my life."

"And your dad never came around?"

"We wouldn't even know how to contact him. Besides, fuck 'im. We were a team and he wasn't on it. I took care of her that summer and fall, forgot about college, and then buried my mom when my friends were heading off to school all over the country. Worst thing that ever happened to me, bro."

"Shit, man. I'm sorry I asked."

I shrugged. "It's okay."

"And no other brothers or sisters or cousins?"

"Mom had an older brother in another state. He never approved much of us. He sent a card when Mom died. Never even came to the funeral."

"Damn."

"Fuck him, too." I realized I was clenching my teeth and made myself relax.

"So how did you pick the Marines?"

"Really wanna know?" I laughed. "I'm such a moron. I was walking in a big mall a few towns over. It was a couple of months after Mom had died, and I was really lonely. I only had a couple of real friends in high school, and they went off to college. I was eighteen, so had to figure out shit in a hurry, you know? All the banking stuff and bills and paying for the funeral and all that shit. Anyway, I had a few hundred dollars set aside and was going to buy myself a Christmas present."

Mack smiled. "Right on. What did you get?"

I chuckled. "So I go to the mall, and I'm just walking around like an idiot shopping for myself. I'd never done that before. Never. Not one time. Mom always got whatever we needed. I mean, sometimes I'd go with her, but I never went alone, ya know? I mean what guy likes to go shopping? So anyway, I'm walking around and I stop to get coffee and see the most beautiful chick I've ever seen—in dress blues."

"No way."

"Toys for Tots. Swear to God. She was a recruiter working at the Toys for Tots booth in the mall. So I walked over and started talking to her. Three things happened after that."

Mack looked up at me from his gun sight and waited.

"First, I saw she was wearing a wedding band, which totally ruined my day. Second, I gave her half my money for Toys for Tots, and third, I took her card for the recruiting office. Shipped November, graduated February. Five months later, I was in Iraq."

After a few minutes, Mack asked, "So what did you get yourself for Christmas?"

"Wasted."

We laughed and gave each other a fist bump.

"It turned out to be a good move. Wasn't much partying on Parris Island or in Iraq."

Mack shook his head and smiled. After a minute he asked, "Were Spade and Squid with you in Iraq?"

"Squid was with me since boot. Spade came later on. But we've been together for a tour in Iraq and now this shithole."

Mack nodded. "It *is* a shithole."

"Roger that. Five months and we get to talk to Geeta."

"Who's Geeta?" asked Mack.

"Geeta fuck outta here!"

Chapter 4

3 June, 2014
Eighteen Days Before "The Incident"
Rip Its

Deke walked into the hooch to find Squid in the fetal position on his rack, wearing boxers only. He was snoring loudly, but looking pale and sweaty. There was a bucket on the floor next to him with some towels, and Spade sat nearby half reading, half keeping an eye on Squid. I pulled off my headphones when I saw Deke.

"What's wrong with Squid?" asked Deke. "He okay?"

"He is definitely *not* okay," I said.

"He is, however, a fucking *warrior!*" screamed Spade, standing up to flex his muscles and roar like a caveman. He held the pose long enough for his muscles to ripple like a bodybuilder.

"And slightly brain damaged," said Mack quietly.

"What happened?" asked Deke.

"Case race," said Spade, beaming with pride.

"No way," replied Deke.

Now, for those folks who never served in today's modern military, an explanation is in order. A *Rip It* is a small can of chemicals and sugar and caffeine and lord-knows-what-else that is consumed by American military personnel of all kinds for one purpose only—to stay awake. I'm guessing you could fit a hundred cups of strong coffee into one Rip It. Drinking more than one at a time is considered foolhardy. Drinking three just isn't recommended at all. Drinking four in one day, well, that just isn't done.

The effects of drinking a Rip It are generally limited to being instantly awake. It can also give you the jitters and even the shakes. Drinking more than one can cause amplification of this to the point of not feeling very well. If you're dumb enough to drink three or four, you've guaranteed yourself horrid shakes, hallucinations, sweating, probably vomiting, and definitely the worst case of the shits you've ever had, other than the one time you ate in some village in Afghanistan before you knew they never washed their hands—like, *ever*.

Now, having explained this, it would be understood that breaking out a case of the offending liquid and racing another person to see who could drink the most the fastest is not a great idea. Known as a "case race", the winner is usually the loser in the long run. Why would anyone do this? Because you're young and dumb, and stuck in the asshole of the world.

Which leads me back to Squid, passed out on his rack.

Deke stared at each of us. "No way."

Spade was still standing like a football coach that had watched a star player score a touchdown. "Yup. He and a few guys from

Third Squad got bored and got into the Rip Its. He ended up drinking eight of them in less than an hour."

"And then shit his brains out," added Mack matter-of-factly.

"And puked," I said.

"And passed out," said Mack.

"And maybe shit himself again, but I ain't checkin'," said Spade.

"You guys are retarded," said Deke.

"Hey man, don't look at me. I learned my lesson last year. Never more than three in a day. Shit, I was hallucinating the first time I did a case race. It was also the last time," said Spade.

"Squid should know better," said Deke.

Mack piped up, "I'm the FNG³, and even *I* know better."

"How long's he been out?" asked Deke.

Spade looked at his watch and made a face. "Maybe an hour. He was trippin' balls for like three hours, then crashed and got sick. We were hanging here babysitting him to make sure he didn't choke to death on his own puke."

"There are *zero* Purple Hearts given out for Rip Its, gentlemen!" snapped Deke.

Mack laughed. "The dude from Third only had seven, then proceeded to shit his brains out in front of Major Clarke!"

Mack and Spade high-fived each other, laughing hysterically.

"It was *classic*, Deke," I explained. "He literally raced out of the hooch, heading straight for the head and screaming in pain, yelling for everyone to get out of his way. He gets like halfway there and literally bumps into Major Clarke and falls down. Before he can get back up, he feels it coming, so he rips his pants down

3 Fucking New Guy

to his knees, right there on the ground, and proceeds to blow a hundred pounds of shit all over the major's boots while he cries and screams like a little girl!"

"Guess that's why they call 'em Rip Its," said Mack, which brought more laughing. Even the sergeant was having a hard time not smiling.

"The major was not happy with him," said Spade.

"Yeah, no kidding," I said. "Major Clarke thinks he has dysentery or something legit, so he calls for a corpsman!" It was hard to talk, I was laughing so hard. "So this dude, King ..."

"I know Matt King," said Deke with a scowl. "Terminal Lance."

"Right," I said, now laughing so hard it was difficult to breathe, "King is lying there hallucinating and moaning, I mean, totally trippin' balls and shittin' his brains out right in the middle of *everyone*, and Doc runs over to him and sees his white sweaty face and checks his hundred-fifty pulse and says calmly to the major, 'This man has a serious case of the Rip Its!'"

All of us were hysterical, other than Deke, who was trying very hard to look like Sergeant Tilman and keep a serious face on.

"What did Major Clarke say?" he asked.

I wiped the tears away and took a breath. "Swear to God, Major Clarke squats down and leans over him and says, 'You ever shit on my boots again and it isn't from drinking local water, a food-borne pathogen, or fucking malaria, and I will personally shoot you in the face.'"

We were roaring. Even Deke couldn't help but start cracking a smile. "Oh shit," he said.

"Shit is the operative word, yes. Doc ended up giving him an IV and putting him in sickbay! He's passed out, too."

Deke shook his head. "Okay, listen, you morons, we have serious shit coming down the pike. Quit fucking around and stay frosty. You need to stay awake? Fine. But don't be chugging that shit like orange Tang. When Squid wakes up, I wanna see him—after he showers. He smells like he was rolling in his own puke."

"He pretty much was," said Spade.

"Jesus, you guys are nasty," snapped Deke. "One more hour tops, then you wake his ass up and throw him in the shower! Then get his lame ass to me. You guys should know better!"

"It wasn't my turn to babysit him," I said.

Deke poked me right in my chest. "He's your best friend! It's *always* your turn to babysit him! You're the corporal, *you* baby-sit *these* morons, and *I* baby-sit *you*!"

Deke tried his best to give us each a hard sergeant stare, but as soon as he stormed off, we could hear him laughing, and we all rolled around on the floor for a few minutes. Squid just lay there shaking and snoring, looking like absolute dog shit. I couldn't stop laughing.

That was a good day.

Chapter 5

4 June, 2014
Seventeen Days Before "The Incident"
Night Ops

Deke walked into the hooch with a pissed-off expression on his face.

"What's up, Sar'int?" I asked.

"Guess who gets to go out tonight in the POS?" he asked.

"Nice," I replied sarcastically. "It's okay, we were getting bored anyway."

"I'm telling you, man, that Humvee's a death machine. I wouldn't even want to drive around in that thing back in the world, never mind here in The Suck."

"What's the status on the Rhino?" I asked him. Our up-armored Rhino was a beast, and had saved us from an IED, but was still awaiting parts for repair. In the meantime, we were stuck driving around in that tin-can Humvee left over from some other war. It had armor, but was nothing at all like the Rhino.

"Who the fuck knows," he grumbled. "Tell the guys. Twenty-two-hundred hours we meet up for the briefing, then head outside the wire to find a goat fucker or two. Major Clarke's leading."

"No shit? Something important?"

"When they tell me, I'll tell you. Spread the word. Eat, shit, and sleep—then ruck up and be ready to roll at twenty-two-hundred." He started to leave then stopped. "Bring extra ammo. If the major's coming, something's up."

"Roger that, Deke."

I went and found the others and spread the word. Squid, Spade, Johnny Mack and I ate together, then geared up and crashed for a few hours. We just lay around half sleeping, shooting the shit. The idea was to sleep before you went out on a night op, but once you were geared up, it was impossible to get real sleep. We were in a shitty part of Ass-Crackistan, and if the major was coming out, it meant we'd be fighting. It would be easier to drink coffee or Rip Its or pop stay-awakes later on than to sleep now, so we just talked and half slept until it was time to go. We met Deke and the LT over at the command tent near the trucks and took seats on whatever we could find, waiting for the brass to come out and tell us what was up.

The LT was a good officer and gave us confidence when we went out that we weren't going to get lost or do something stupid. We'd been out with him dozens of times and had only had three casualties in six months. In this part of The Shit, that was considering extremely lucky. We all exchanged greetings and were talking when Deke barked, "Attention on deck!"

We jumped up and watched Major Clarke walk out of the command tent with an "As you were." He told us all to find seats. His briefing was short and to the point. We were heading out to a nearby village to find some goat fucker named Mohammed. The whole country was named Mohammed. This particular

Mohammed had been making IEDs that were fucking up our people. If the intel was correct, which only happened half the time, we'd wake his ass up at the point of a gun and bring him in alive. If he resisted or we took fire, we were cleared to engage with deadly force. Rah.

We all piled into our truck and headed out, following the major in his Rhino. Nobody said anything about the fact that the major had an up-armored Rhino and we were in the death machine since the major was actually going out into The Shit with us, something that didn't happen very often. If Major Clarke was going to embrace The Suck *with* us, he could have the good truck.

It was a forty-minute drive through pitch-black dirt roads when the convoy stopped and everyone un-assed the truck. Our fire team joined two others to make up our squad. The major seemed like he was more "along for the ride" than directing the operation, but my gut told me everything had been carefully coordinated with the LT before they left. Major Clarke was quiet and observant as the LT and the sergeants had everyone move out towards the village on foot. We all had night vision goggles and entered silently with total stealth.

The LT directed the sergeant to the stone shithole that was the target's house, and the sergeant moved his fire team up into position. How they knew one stone shithole from another was beyond me. They all looked exactly alike. Maybe that's why the Hajis don't drink—they'd never be able to find their way to the right house at the end of the night.

It was that five minutes or so before hitting a target that was always the most difficult for me. The waiting seemed like forever.

The adrenaline was pumping, but you had to be silent, which meant your urge to scream and charge into the mud huts and stone shitholes had to be kept in check. We moved in total silence, using hand signals. Team Two was Assault, in charge of breaching the house. We were Support behind the house, where we had slipped over a short stone fence. Team Three was across the street with the LT and Major Clarke, setting up Security and cordoning off the approach to the target house.

What happened next was a little unclear. I'm not sure if the dogs started barking and alerted the Hajis inside, or the gunfire started and then the dogs went crazy. All I know is, it was silent one second, and then total chaos the next. Team Two had just moved through the doorway when everything went south. In a split second, the team was fully engaged, the dogs went ape-shit, and we were running across the rear yard towards the house.

When the house exploded, it knocked all of us on our asses and lit up the night sky. The secondary explosions continued for a few seconds, pinning us down, and then a steady rain of rocks and dirt started coming down on us. Holy shit.

Before I caught my breath, Chuckie Spade was up and running towards the house with his M240 at the ready. My head was ringing so badly I could barely see, never mind run. By the time my team was all reorganized and arrived at what had been the house, it was over. The house was destroyed, and Team Two was gone. Like—totally gone. All five Marines were just taken apart. The two corpsmen went body to body, but it was useless. The house had been filled with explosives, and the Mohammed we were hunting had detonated something right when Team Two hit the house. He and whoever was in the house with him went up in a flash along with our five brothers.

Welcome to The Suck.

We ended up on site until the sun came up, going house to house rounding up goat fuckers and having our interpreter interrogate everyone. The general consensus seemed to be that Mohammed was Taliban and everyone was too scared of him to do anything about his activities. The rest of the village was made up of dirt-poor farmers who hadn't ever been more than five klicks from their village in their whole life. The major had our Afghan interpreter take one of the villagers with us, but the terrified guy seemed clueless.

Our mission to prevent future IED attacks and thereby save lives ended up killing five of our men. Would those IEDs have done even more damage? Probably. But that sure as hell didn't make it seem any better to us. The drive home was mostly in silence. Squid had been good friends with a kid in Team Two and took it the hardest. He had driven on the way out, but Mack drove back to base. Squid sat in the back, face to the wall, crying most of the way home.

There was so much we all wanted to say.

And no one said a word.

Chapter 6

10 June, 2014
Eleven Days Before "The Incident"

The week after the night op was mostly "time off." My fire team had all been concussed by the explosion and the doc had given us five days of light duty. We weren't sent back to Camp Leatherneck, we just hung around in the brutal heat of Patrol Base Boldak. I think it was more "mercy" break than medical. The PB[4] was quiet and everyone was looking pretty gray. There had been a ceremony on base for Team Two, and their boots, M4s, Kevlar covers, and dog tags had been stationed in a small memorial. The general mood was shit.

By the tenth of June, the heat was getting wicked during the day. The Rhino was still waiting for parts, which meant more time in the Humvee with the shitty air-conditioner and second-rate armor. Major Clarke had personally come to visit each of us, which I thought was pretty classy on his part. He seemed to actually give a shit about his people, and his kindness was genuine.

---

4 PB, Patrol Base – In Afghanistan, FOBs (Forward Operating Bases) and PB (Patrol Bases) are small encampments typically supported by larger Main Operating Bases. Patrol Bases serve as remote outposts from which patrols can be run. Living conditions are primitive at best.

I guess he felt partly responsible for the five KIAs, not that we could have done anything any differently, other than just drop a few tons of ordnance from a B-52, which had been *my* suggestion for the whole fucking country six months ago.

I walked into the tent we called "home" and found my bunkmate Squid on his computer. He was sitting on the bottom rack where he slept, Skyping with his little sister, the fifteen-year-old.

"Hey, Sean—say hey to Abby." He turned the laptop around and there was his little sister's face. Her smile lit up our otherwise shitty tent. She was fifteen, and I knew she had a little crush on me. I plopped down next to Squid on his rack.

"Hey there, Little Squid! What time is it back in the world? Shouldn't you be asleep?"

"It's only midnight."

"You have school tomorrow!"

"School sucks."

"Yeah, well, you better do good in school or they'll send your ass out here to Ass-Crackistan with us."

She smiled, her big brown eyes twinkling. "That wouldn't be so bad …"

Uh-oh. Squid shot me a serious look. "She's *fifteen*, dude …" he whispered.

I laughed. "Good to see you, Abby. Go to bed! You better get straight A's!"

Squid turned the laptop back around and gave his sister a kiss. "Love ya, kiddo. Say hi to Mom and Dad for me." They signed off and he closed the laptop. He got choked up for no particular reason, then took a long, slow breath. Squid had been way down since we lost Team Two. It was good that he had a few minutes with his sister.

"She looks great, man."

"You better behave."

"I didn't mean like *that*, you dick. She's a little kid. Just nice to see a smiling face is all."

He nodded and very quietly agreed. "Yeah." He looked at me, and his face changed. "Hey man." His voice caught for a second. "Anything ever happens to me, you gotta go see her in person. Tell her what happened."

"What the fuck, dude?" I exclaimed.

"I'm serious, man."

"Squid. Nothing's gonna happen. Chill the fuck out, man."

He leaned closer and hissed through clenched teeth, "*Promise me*. Anything ever happens, you go see my family. Abby would be all kinds of fucked up. She's just a kid."

I knew he was hurting. If promising him would make him feel better, so be it. "Sure, man. Anything happens to you, I'll go in person. I promise. Okay?"

He gave me a fist bump and leaned back on his rack. "This place sucks."

"You just noticing now?" I asked him.

He cleared his throat and sat back up on the edge of his bed. He sat there, elbows on his knees, hands clasped, looking pensive. "You know, after my uncle died in the Tower, I just wanted to join the Marines and kill the fuckers responsible. Plain and simple. Just some payback for all our people, you know? But shit, man. These people are barely worth killing. Half the fuckers still think they're fighting the Russians. They don't even know what 9/11 was. Most of them can't read, have no idea where America is, and have never left their fucking village. Why the fuck're we even here, man? The goat fucker that blew up that house killed five of our guys. If we just left this shithole country and went home, what threat does he pose to America? He's only a threat here. Fuck 'em."

I made a face. "This does *not* sound like the John Wayne Squid muthafucker I know and love. You had a Bronze Star for valor in forty days. Now you're ready to quit and go home?"

He stared right through me and simply said, "Yeah."

It was like being gut-punched. "Shit, dude. Don't say that. Team One needs your badassness. Don't get all negative on me, man."

He shrugged. "Fuck it," he mumbled and laid down, making me stand up.

"Man, I still got a fucking headache," I said as the pain reappeared from my concussion.

"Yeah, me, too. I think only Spade feels normal because his skull's so fucking thick."

I smiled. That sounded more like the Squid I knew. "It's gonna be a hundred and ten today. Deke says we're humping ten klicks on foot."

Squid shot up in bed. "You fucking with me?"

"Yup."

He threw a pair of socks at me. "Asshole."

"Ahh, see? You're feeling better already."

Chapter 7

Up to 21 June

The days before "my incident of twenty-one June" were depressing and hot. We stayed on PB Boldak trying to kill time doing anything we could. We caught rays, took naps, wrote emails, worked out, cleaned weapons, and tried not to walk past the memorial to our lost fire team too many times.

On the twentieth, I was up early for no particular reason and decided to get coffee and just watch the sunrise. Mornings were usually quiet and kind of poetic in the desert, when you weren't getting mortared or shot at. I was walking by myself, drinking coffee and letting myself wake up slowly—a real luxury, when I heard a familiar grunting.

I followed the noise to the small area where we kept all the weights and the weight bench. It was fairly common for guys to lift to stay in shape and kill time, but not at this hour. I walked over and stood leaning against a blast wall, watching the largest human being on base bench pressing. I'm pretty sure Spade had all the weights on the base on the bar. Walking over to spot him would have been a waste of time. If he couldn't lift it up, neither could I.

I watched, sipping coffee in silence as his arms cranked out reps like a machine. Giant pistons instead of human arms, cranking up and down. After a while, I realized that Spade was crying and cursing under his breath as he just kept going. I have no idea how many reps he'd done, but it was insane. The sweat ran down his arms, and every vein was popping. Finally, I walked quietly behind him in the spotter's position and whispered, "Okay, big man, let's give it a break."

Spade was on a different planet—under some spell. When he heard my voice, the spell was broken and he had to struggle to get the weight bar back on the rack. I used every muscle in my body to help lift it to the resting rack, but it was mostly for moral support.

"Jesus, dude. How many did you do?"

Spade lay on the bench, eyes closed with sweat pouring out of him. His shirt was off, and I just stared in awe at the beast. After he caught his breath, he said, still panting, "The NFL record at the combine was fifty-one reps. Two hundred twenty-five pounds as many times as you can. That's how it works. Less than twenty guys in NFL history broke forty."

"How many did you do?"

"Last one doesn't count—you helped ..."

"Bullshit, dude. I barely touched it. How many?"

"That was sixty. So, fifty-nine."

"God *damn*, Spade!"

"I can't lift my arms," he whispered, still completely out of breath.

I stared at his face. Mixed in with the sweat I could swear I was watching tears. "You okay? I mean, you injure yourself just now?"

Spade opened his eyes and stared at me, and then I was sure he was crying. Tears were just running down the sides of his thick skull.

"Val emailed me," he managed to croak.

"Oh shit." I knew the deal the second he opened his mouth.

"Too far away. Gone too long. You know the deal." His voice cracked ever so slightly. He wiped his face with his hand. More of a paw than a human hand.

"Shit. Sorry, bro. Come on, let's get you up."

"I can't fuckin' move, bro. I think I'm having a heart attack."

"Fuck that. You didn't come to The Suck to die of a heart attack. We'll go like *Vikings*. Come on."

I walked around and stuck out my hand, leaning way back to help hoist the beast. Together, we stood him up and he leaned against the blast wall. The guy was a perfect human specimen. "Yo, man. When we get home, you gotta go try and get back into football. You'd make millions in the NFL. Don't let anyone tell you your knee doesn't work. I've seen you carry a hundred twenty pounds in a hundred twenty degrees for ten klicks. *Sheeeit*. The NFL would be a cakewalk."

He cracked a smile. "That ship has sailed, my man. Just like Val. A fuckin' *email*. You believe that shit? Three years together and not even the decency of a Skype or something. Just a six-sentence email."

His head rolled back against the wall and he closed his eyes, totally exhausted. "I thought we'd get married, you know?"

I smacked his arm. "Ruck up. Her loss. Next time we get some R&R, I'm going to buy you a beautiful goat to call your own. Unless you're more of a camel guy. I can probably get you a camel. Extra virgin."

"Thanks. You're all heart."

He straightened up and looked at me, his face serious. "Don't say nuthin', okay? I'll tell the guys when I feel like it."

"Rah."

We just stood there for a second, both of us feeling a million miles from anyplace decent. The Suck wasn't particularly good for relationships. We averaged about one ruined romance a week on Boldak.

"You good?"

"Yeah. Gonna shit, shower, and shave. Catch you at the hooch. And thanks."

He grabbed his t-shirt and walked away to clean up. I looked at the weights and thought about seeing how many I could do, then decided I didn't want to be found dead with a weight bar across my throat. I drank my coffee and returned to the hooch.

By the time we got orders to go back out in the POS Humvee, we actually wanted to go just to get off base and do *something*. I kept thinking, maybe blowing something up would be therapeutic. It might have been, had "the thing blowing up" not been me and my battle buddies in that Humvee. Twenty-one June. In a shithole in the middle of nowhere that no one back home would ever hear of, and I'd never see again.

Explosions.

Screaming.

My friends burning.

Deke running and shooting and saving my sorry ass from the middle of a baked dirt road.

Then … nothing.

Chapter 8
Walter Reed

The trip from Afghanistan to the hospital ship by chopper, and then to Germany by plane was a haze. The medical staff was kind enough to keep me unconscious most of the trip. I remember now waking up here and there, and having very nice folks talk to me and pat my hands and tell me I was going to be fine, but that's about it. I didn't remember most of it for months.

I can remember at one point being in a room, surrounded by other guys who all looked as fucked up as I was. It was a surreal scene. I mean, I *think* it was real. I just remember clothes being cut off of Marines, and blood and black, burned skin and body parts coming off and occasional screaming. Doctors and nurses were shouting orders and running around. There was *so* much blood. I was getting lifted up and moved around a lot, I think. I remember an Asian-looking doctor looking down on me and speaking in a very soothing voice, telling me I had been injured badly and would lose my leg, but he was going to save my life. I think he said he was sorry about my leg. I still see bits and pieces of all that when I have my nightmares. I can see that doctor's rubber gloves, slick with blood. My blood. It was everywhere.

From the time the doctor spoke to me to the time I woke up in Germany, I don't remember anything else. Germany was a blur, and they told me I'd be going State-side. I slept the entire flight and for days after in a medically induced coma. I just remember waking up in Walter Reed Medical Center in a very white bed with very white sheets and white blankets. The ceiling was white. The fluorescent tubes gave off a white glow. The walls and floor were white. The curtain was white. White *everything*.

It was so quiet and I was on a lot of drugs, so I wasn't very clear-headed, but my first thought was, "I'm dead."

"I'm dead and I'm in Heaven ..."

I could feel my chest collapsing and it was getting harder to breathe. Was God going to come see me? Saint Peter? I never went to church much. Would I even get in? I called out into the whiteness.

"Hello? Is anyone here? Am I dead?"

I kept blinking and trying to focus, and felt pain in my legs. I looked down and saw the stump of my right leg, wrapped heavily in bandages.

"Oh God ..."

Everything started crashing down on me. The explosion. The incoming rocket-propelled grenades and tracer rounds. The screaming. It had been *my* screaming. My leg. I started crying and couldn't stop until I felt a hand on my shoulder.

A calm voice said, "Welcome back to the world."

"Deke?"

I had never been so happy to see another human being in my life. If I could just stop crying.

"Easy, bro. Take it slow," he said.

"I thought I was dead. Everything was white and no one was here. I thought that was it."

"No way, bro. You made it."

I stared at Deke, remembering in a foggy haze how he'd charged out into the road and pulled me behind the wall. How he stood over me, firing his weapon, with his hot shells raining down on me in slow motion.

"You were fucking Superman, Deke."

"We look out for each other, right?"

"Squid, Johnny Mack, and The Spade okay?"

Deke shook his head, looking sad.

"Deke?"

"Sorry, bro. That piece of shit Humvee hit a fat girl. Probably an Explosively Formed Projectile. They never made it out."

"*All* of them?" I asked, trying to remember everything.

"Yeah. Sorry, Nicky. It was instant. You were thrown out of the truck."

I thought back to the POS Humvee. The air conditioner sucked, and I had opened my door just a crack to try and breathe before I roasted alive in there. I'd been blown out the open door.

"My leg ..." I said quietly.

"Yeah. I'm sorry about that, too, man. There was nothing we could do to save it. It was just gone."

"Is it still there?" I asked.

"No, man. It's gone. See?" He pointed at my stump with his chin.

"No," I said. "I mean, in Afghanistan. Did it just get left there?"

"I guess so, yeah."

I stared at my stump. "I guess it doesn't matter, right?"

Deke rubbed my shoulder. "Your leg? No, man. You're still here. That's all that matters."

"And Squid? And Spade? And Mack? That's it?"

"I'm sorry, man. There was nothing I could do for them," he replied, his voice cracking as the tears came.

"You were like Superman. You saved my life, Deke."

"Couldn't help the others, though," he said quietly.

"IEDs," I mumbled. "The whole fucking country is just one big IED."

Deke patted my shoulder. "You're gonna be okay, though. Gonna have a lot of stuff to deal with, you know? More surgery. Maybe a few more. Then you have to get fitted for a leg and learn to walk again. It's gonna take a while. But you'll be running again in no time." He forced a smile.

"Yeah, but not with Squid," I said before even realizing it came out of my mouth.

"It was a clusterfuck," said Deke quietly.

"You think it's just lying on the side of the road?" I asked.

"Your leg?"

"Yeah."

He shrugged. "I don't know. Don't think about that, man. You're alive. You made it."

"I know. 'Cause of you. Superman. Still. It shouldn't just be lying there. It's mine, you know? What if some dogs got it or something?"

Deke shook his head. "You gotta let it go, man. Listen. After we got medevac'd, the major called in an airstrike. That road, the village, half the fucking mountain—they're just *gone*, man. Your leg's gone, okay? We left a big black fucking hole. That's it. A big fucking hole."

I tried to relax. Deke saw that I was looking tired and a bit overwhelmed and said, "You need to sleep."

I grabbed his hand. "Hey. We gotta go see 'em."

"Who? See *who*, Sean?"

"Their families. I promised Squid. I gotta go see Abby."

"Okay. You just sleep for now. I'll come see you soon, and we'll figure it all out. Right now, you just got to get better."

I stared up into the lights. "I thought I was dead, Deke ..."

I might have nodded off for a second. When I looked back for Deke, he was gone. I lay there in silence, feeling a little better after talking to him, and a nurse walked in. She was surprised to see me just lying there, wide awake.

"Well, hello there, Corporal Nichols," she said cheerfully. "Do you know where you are?" She walked over and began rubbing my hands with hers. They were very warm. It made me think of my mom. She used to rub my hands when I was little, coming in from outside in winter. Then I used to rub hers after chemo when she was cold and sick.

"I thought I was dead," I whispered.

"Nope. You're very much alive. You got hurt pretty bad, Sean. But you're going to be fine. Do you know where you are?"

"Back in the world," I said, feeling light-headed.

"Correct. You're in Walter Reed Medical Center. In Maryland." She was pressing the call button. "You understand, Sean?"

"Yeah. My leg."

She kept rubbing and patting my hands, helping to chase away the cobwebs. She played with some tubes that were attached to me and wiped my face with a cool rag.

"The doctor will be here soon. You're going to be okay, Sean. You're alive. You have an alive day. A new birthday. Twenty-one June. It's hard, I know, but we're going to help you, I promise."

A doctor walked in wearing green scrubs. He looked to be in his forties maybe. A nice-looking guy with a big smile and warm blue eyes. The nurse smiled at him and said, "Doctor McGloughlin, Sean just woke up. Sean, this is Doctor McGloughlin."

"Sean, welcome home," he said calmly. His voice was somehow very reassuring and helped with the panicky feeling in my chest. "I was your surgeon here at Walter Reed. You've had two surgeries already. Do you remember anything? Are you in any pain?"

"No." I said. And then blurted, "My leg's in Afghanistan."

The doctor shot a look at the nurse, and she adjusted the morphine drip.

"We're going to get you fitted for a new leg soon, Sean. You need to heal first. You're going to get out of that bed today, and in a few days you're going to be walking on your own with crutches. There are a lot of really good people here to help you, Sean."

I don't know why, but at that moment, the crying started and wouldn't stop. "They got Mack and Squid and Spade! They got 'em all!" I cried. The tears were flowing like a busted dam.

The nurse leaned over and held my hands in hers. "I know it's really hard, Sean. I know. It gets easier with time, I promise."

"Deke and I need to go visit their families. I promised Squid."

"When you're up and around, you can visit anyone you want. Is there anyone you want us to contact? You had no contact information in your file. Do you have family?"

"Just Deke," I said. Squid, Mack and Spade were all gone. "No one to call."

"I'm going to get you some food. You haven't eaten anything in days."

"How long I been out?" I asked.

"Five days, on and off. Do you remember the trip?"

"I thought I was dead."

"You're alive. Let me get you some food."

The doc leaned over and smiled. "The food's so bad you'll know you're not in Heaven. You're going to be fine, son. I promise."

"There was a lot of screaming," I said to the nurse, still processing her other question about the trip. "That was me. I was the one screaming. My leg …"

The doc listened to my chest and took my pulse.

"There was a different doc. He said he was sorry my leg was gone. He couldn't save my leg, but he'd save my life. Yeah. I remember now. There were other guys in there, too. Everybody was *so fucked up*." I looked at the nurse. "Sorry."

"I've heard worse," she said with a smile. She was sweet.

The doctor patted my arm. "Get some food in your belly. Just some soup at first. Real slow, Sean. You haven't had real food in your belly all week. Take it slow. I'll come back and see you soon."

And then I had soup.

I was alive.

You had to be alive to have soup.

Chapter 9
Walter Reed

I woke up to the sound of screaming and crying. I looked around and tried to see who was making so much fucking noise. It was me. I'd been having a nightmare. The nurse appeared magically and rubbed my arm. She shushed me and soothed me in a mom voice that took the darkness away, and my heart rate slowed.

"Easy baby, easy baby," she kept saying. I apologized for screaming like a lunatic.

"It's okay, it happens around here from time to time. It's early. Get some rest."

I fell back to sleep.

When I woke up the second time, Deke was standing over me in a sunlit room.

"Hey! What are you doing here?" I said when I saw him. He smiled and held my shoulder.

"I told you last time I'd be back," he replied.

"Man, I barely remember last time," I said. "I mean, now that you say it, yeah, I remember seeing you. But man, I was out of it."

"You look a lot better."

"Thanks. I feel a lot better. I think I was high out of my mind last time you saw me. I've been up walking every day since you were here. When was that? A week ago?"

"Almost. But you're doing great."

"Not so much. First couple times they made me get up, the blood rushes down to the stump, you know? Pain was unfuckingbelievable. I pissed myself, dude. You have no idea how fucked up this is."

"Baby steps, man. You're going to be fine. I know it hurts."

"Are *you* okay? I mean, you're not in the hospital for you, are you?"

"No, I just came to see you."

"I keep thinking about my leg on the side of the road in Ass-Crackistan. I wish I could get it. I know it sounds ridiculous, but it's mine, ya know?"

Deke stared at me and shook his head. I felt like an idiot. "I know, I know," I said apologetically. "What would I do with it? Put it over the fireplace someday when I get a house?"

"You're seriously brain damaged," said Deke.

I waved it off. My mind went from my leg to the ambush and Deke saving me again, and I remembered seeing him standing over me.

"Hey. I remember seeing you get hit! You okay?"

"Like you said, 'Superman.'"

"It's like a dream, Deke. I see your shell casing fall in slow motion. The corpsman was screaming, but I couldn't hear anything. Fucking tracers everywhere like wasps. What a mess."

"Clusterfuck," Deke agreed.

"Nurse told me I've got a guy coming to talk to me about prosthetics."

"Yeah, I can't stay. You have a busy day ahead of you. Just came by to check in."

"You coming back?"

"I'll be around."

"How much time off you get?"

"Dude, they gave me a Silver Star for saving your ass. I have all the time in the world."

I smiled. I was glad Deke was at least recognized for his bravery. He sure saved my ass.

"I gotta go. You ain't supposed to have visitors yet. Good luck today." And with that, he gave me a quick fist bump and left.

I was lying in bed doing a whole lot of nothing when a very large black man entered my room. He had sergeant major written all over him. A shaved head and chiseled face sat on top of a thick neck and giant shoulders. The T-shirt, stretched tight over his massive chest, read RANGERS LEAD THE WAY. It took me a second to realize he was standing on two prosthetic legs. The man was a beast, fake legs or not.

"Good morning, Devil Dog," he barked. I swear, he had to be a drill sergeant at one time in his career.

"Morning," I managed to muster.

"Staff Sergeant Darryl Robbins, Seventy-Fifth Ranger Regiment. Currently retired due to a slight injury, but now two inches taller." He pointed to my good leg. "See, *you* got screwed. If you only lose one, they can't make you taller."

I couldn't help but smile. "Guess not. You seriously gave yourself an extra inch?"

"Two inches. Pay attention. Marine." He shook his head in mock disgust. "See, they ask you how tall you were before you got hurt, and if you're quick on your feet … see what I did there? You can just tell them anything. I said I was six-two. Fuck 'em. I hope they're paying by the inch, too."

"Yeah, but now your clothes won't fit," I replied, trying to be a wise ass.

"True. Smart kid. See, I wasn't that smart. Didn't realize the problem I had created until I was discharged and nothing fit. Oh well. I wear shorts now most of the time anyway to let you new guys see that you'll be up and around soon. And you will. So whatever thoughts you have about blowing your brains out, or feeling sorry for yourself, you just dump that shit, hear?"

"I'm not suicidal. Hell, Deke worked too hard to save my ass."

He smiled, a huge toothy grin, and shook my hand with his massive paw. "And *that*, son, is the proper attitude to have! A lot of very good doctors and nurses worked very hard to keep your ass on this side of the sod. You owe it to them and yourself to get your ass out of this bed and do something with yourself. Your goals are simple at the moment. Allow your body to heal and your stump to shrink. Get fitted for a new leg and learn to walk on it. One day, you'll be running on it, if that's your thing. Eight weeks or so from the time you returned from the dead, and you'll be starting your new life."

I thought about my long runs with Squid. "I've been out of bed a lot. Haven't had a fitting yet."

"Yeah, the stump has to heal. Takes a while. And get used to calling it that. It's a *stump*, not a leg. You have to face facts. It needs to stay wrapped real tight to help it heal and shrink so we can get you fitted. Anyone here talk to you about HO yet? Heterotopic ossification?

That didn't sound so good. "No."

"Yeah, something else to look forward to. Here's the deal. Your leg bones want to heal. Thinks it can grow a new leg. It can't. But you can end up with bone growth in your muscle tissue, sometimes into your skin. Hurts like a bitch. That's down the road, maybe six months or a year out. Sometimes means another surgery, even a new prosthetic. Don't want to freak you out, but you have to be aware of the possibilities."

"So they had to cut your legs again?" I asked, grimacing.

"I was lucky. Had some problems with the right leg, no problems with the left. The repair was manageable, just added some time to rehab, that's all. Hurt like a *bitch*, though. Just something to keep in mind if you start getting bad pain some months down the road. Listen to your body. You seen your x-rays yet?"

I hadn't.

"Well, you take a good luck when you can. Check for the shrapnel so you know where it is. Your skin's gonna be spitting out pieces of metal and rocks and who-knows-what for the next fifty years. You think you have a big zit or something, and the next thing you know, you're pulling a nail out of your thigh. The Hajis use whatever they can get to make bombs and fuck us up. It gets interesting."

"So you came here just to cheer me up today, huh?" I asked.

"Nope. I came here to bring you down to the lab for your first fitting. I work here. I'm going to be your worst nightmare and best friend, but I promise you, you *will* walk out of here without crutches."

Darryl shook my hand with a vice-like grip and looked straight into my brain. Straight-shooting, no-bullshit guy. I liked him already. I managed to say a timid, "Deal."

Chapter 10
Walter Reed

Waking up from a nightmare wasn't anything new. Waking up not being able to scream or breathe was.

I woke up choking and coughing up dark frothy blood, and my chest felt like it was collapsing on me. I tried to scream, but nothing would come out. I'm not sure how I managed it, pure survival instinct I guess, but I grabbed the call button and started pounding on it. It was the first time I'd ever used it, and I guess it was a good thing the nurses weren't used to seeing my room monitor buzzing.

By the time the nurse came in, I was sure I was dying. I couldn't breathe and I felt my life ending. It seemed so lame to me, to survive the ambush, and then die from "nothing" weeks later. As the lights started to go out, I could hear the nurse screaming at the top of her lungs. She was telling me to try and relax and breathe as she screamed into her radio that she needed a doctor in 1215 stat.

By the time the doc came in, I was turning purple and sliding under a huge dark wave of pain. I sort of remember the doc talking to me, asking if my chest hurt, if I could breathe. Dumb-ass questions. As he listened to my chest, he was shouting instructions to the worried-looking nurse.

"Heart rate elevated. Let's get him to x-ray immediately. I want Heparin, ten thousand units stat! And tell OR to prepare for a pulmonary embolism. Find Dr. Richmond and have him meet me in OR!"

Next thing I knew, orderlies were pushing my bed down the hall at a run. We passed right by Deke, who raised his hand and sort of waved at me. He was screaming at me, "Hang in there, Sean! Just breathe, baby! Just breathe! You're gonna be okay!"

Then the lights went out.

When I woke up, Deke was standing over me, his hand reassuringly on my shoulder. He smiled as I opened my eyes. I felt like shit.

"Welcome back to the land of the living," he said quietly.

My first attempt at speech came out as a croak. There was an oxygen line under my nose, and my throat and lips were so dry I couldn't talk. I managed to pull the tube down off my nose and ask Deke what happened.

"Pulmonary embolism. Blood clot from your leg traveled to your lung. Not that uncommon with your injuries. Dangerous, though."

"So you're a doctor now, too?" I asked him weakly.

"I do it all, baby," he said with his usual smile.

"How long was I out?"

"Just overnight. It's morning."

"How long you been here?"

"The whole time, brother. Think I would bail out on you when you needed someone looking over you?"

"I feel like shit," I croaked.

"You'll be fine. Two days, tops, and you'll be good to go. Just be careful shaving." He smiled again, looking like a wiseass.

"Huh?"

"You cut yourself right now, you'll bleed out. They got enough blood thinner in you to drop a pony."

"Deke ..."

"Yeah?"

"Thanks, man."

Deke, never the mushy type, leaned over and kissed my forehead, like he was my dad or something. He whispered, "I got your six, Nicky. *Always.*"

He stayed right where he was, holding my shoulder, until I felt the sleep coming for me like a weight pulling me under water. I had someone guarding the perimeter for me though, so I let myself fall into a very deep sleep.

When I woke up, I was confused and still pretty out of it. It took me a second to piece together what had happened. I looked up and spotted Deke leaning against the wall, looking at me. He smiled and said, "Hey, champ."

"Hey. When did you get here?"

"I've *been* here. You were racked out."

"I think all I do is sleep."

"Yeah, well, your body has a lot of healing to do. You might not remember, but you were blown up. You're about to have a *really* shitty day."

"Why?"

"Scrub day."

"What's that mean?" I asked, feeling a little scared.

Deke came closer and leaned over me, close to my face. He whispered, "In a few minutes, a very nice nurse is gonna come in here and show you what looks like steel wool. She's gonna use it to clean the end of your stump. You are *not* going to enjoy the experience. It'll be over before you know it, though. Ruck up, Marine. Set your jaw and try not to embarrass us." He patted my shoulder then leaned next to my ear and whispered, "It's okay to cry, sometimes. I'll be back tomorrow. Good luck, brother."

He turned and walked out, and I called after him to stay, now feeling somewhat terrified. He just waved his hand and kept walking. A few minutes later, a very pretty nurse walked in pushing a cart.

"Hey there, sunshine," she said, faking a smile.

"Steel wool day?" I asked.

"And have you been out and about asking 'what happens next questions' around the ward?"

"A birdie whispered in my ear," I told her.

"Well, we can't allow necrosis or blistering …"

"Necrosis?" I asked. Whatever that was, it didn't sound good.

"Necrosis is dead tissue. It can lead to infection. The skin at the wound site is very tender, but I need to clean the area. This won't feel so good."

"Do what you gotta do," I said, trying my very best to sound like a battle-hardened Marine. I could feel myself getting sick to my stomach just thinking about her scrubbing my stump, which already hurt without even touching it.

She smiled and began organizing her "stuff" on the cart. "If it gets to be too much, you just say so and we'll take a break, or I can give you some pain meds."

"Enough with the meds," I said. "My brain is gonna be fried. Just get it over with. Don't stop—just get it done as fast as you can, okay?"

And then the torture started. I kept telling myself that it was standard procedure that every amputee had to face. They'd all survived. Darryl had to have two legs done. I'd survive. I covered my face with my pillow and screamed into it as she apologized and scrubbed off weeks of scabbing, debris, and God-knows-what-else. I was sweating right through the sheets by the time she was done.

When it was over, she patted my chest and told me I was a hard-ass Marine. It's all I could ask for. She rewrapped my stump, which I didn't look at for fear of what I'd see, and then helped me throw on a new shirt since I had sweated through the last one. I asked her if she was going to help with my shorts, to which she smiled and said, "Nice try."

After she left, I flopped back on the bed and almost fainted. I think I slept five hours. When I opened my eyes, Deke was standing there, looking concerned.

"Hey. How you doing?" he asked softly.

"You weren't shittin'. About the steel wool, I mean."

"Yeah. Sorry it sucked so bad."

"Embrace The Suck," I quoted. "It's better now. Just tender. Are you AWOL or something? How'd you get so much time off?"

"I told you! I got a Silver Star says I can do whatever I want. Don't you worry about me, I got all the time in the world, brother. Just get some rest and prepare yourself for learning how to walk again. It's going to be challenging. You're a Marine. Suck it up. I gotta go, you got shit to do. Ooh Rahh …"

"Wait …" But he was gone again.

Chapter 11
On Your Foot, Soldier

Shortly after Deke left, Darryl walked in. Something about that guy—every time he walked in I felt like I needed to jump up and stand at attention.

"Guess what day it is, Marine?" he barked.

"Milkshake Day?"

"You wish. It's 'Get Off Your Sorry Ass And Stop Feeling Sorry For Yourself Day.' You're getting a new leg today, Marine. You ready?"

"Ready as I'm gonna be," I said.

"Not quite the level of enthusiasm I was looking for from a United States Marine. *You ready?*" he barked, like I was back at Parris Island.

I gave him a serious "Ooohhh Raahh!"

He smiled and his face softened. When he opened his arms wide and said *"See?"* his whole demeanor changed. He grabbed my braces and helped me up onto my one foot. "On your *foot*, Marine!" he barked, then gave me an evil smile.

"One more than *you* got, Staff Sergeant," I said coolly.

"Damn, son. That's some cold shit. Let's go. Please try to keep up."

I walked after him the best I could. He was busting my chops the whole walk to the elevator. "Come on, Devil Dog! Wheelchairs are for people who need 'em! Keep up for God's sakes, you're embarrassing the Corps!"

We took the elevator down to another floor, and he walked me to a small "lab" where specialists fitted me for my new right leg. I even watched a short movie by the company that made the prosthetic. If nothing else, the movie had me believing I'd be up and running one day soon. I was pretty pumped up by the time it was over. That is, right up until the part where they slid my very sensitive stump into the prosthetic and began making adjustments. Yeah. It hurt.

Once I was literally on two feet, they brought me to some parallel bars and had me walk for the first time on my new leg. There were a lot of very encouraging, smiling faces in that room, and I felt truly blessed to live in a country where a new leg was even a possibility. I know the Hajis weren't getting shit when they got blown up. But fuck 'em.

The first few steps were agonizing. Allowing my body weight into the stump was brutal. But I walked.

I *walked*.

Chapter 12
Rehab

Darryl was right about a lot of things. He was my best friend, other than Deke, and my worst enemy. There were days he made me cry—well, he and the rehab nurses and docs. He was also right about my body pushing out stuff that didn't belong there.

I remember one morning waking up in a dirty bed. Dirty, as in *dirt*. I felt like I was sitting in crumbs. I just kept brushing off little bits of sand and rocks from my bed, feeling confused. Had someone emptied their shoes out on my bed? I finally sat up, put on my new leg and stood up out of bed on my own. When I looked at my bottom sheet, it was covered in little spots of blood and pieces of all kinds of crap. I examined my legs and found about a hundred little scabs. My ass and stomach and back, too. While I was sleeping, my skin had decided it was time to push out whatever had been imbedded into it on twenty-one June. I stared at my bed. It was full of Afghanistan. I ripped off the sheets and threw them into a corner of the room. Fuck Afghanistan. I didn't want that shit anywhere near me.

Darryl walked in as I was cursing at the pile of sheets in some kind of juvenile temper tantrum.

"Have a problem with the quality of your thread count or something?" he asked.

"Woke up lying in Afghanistan dirt. Didn't like it."

"Ahh," he mumbled. "Now that, I understand. Least you aren't *buried* in it. Come on. We're going outside for a walk."

I couldn't help but smile. Since I'd been hurt, I hadn't been outside hardly at all. A couple of times in a wheelchair, but that was it. I was beyond excited.

"Oh look!" he exclaimed, once again busting my balls. "It smiles!"

We ended up walking almost a half mile outside. It was hot and sunny and felt so good I had a hard time fighting back the tears. He could tell, but had a way of knowing when to bust my balls and when to just be a friend. He patted me on the back and told me how to improve my gait, work on my posture, use my core muscles—how to walk like everyone else. Including him, on two prosthetic legs. Darryl was nothing short of inspiring. We took a break on a bench and took in our surroundings. There were a lot of families around with their injured loved ones. I saw a lot of men and women who were in way worse shape than me.

Darryl snapped me out of my thoughts. "You've come a long way, Sean."

"Yeah. Afghanistan seems like another lifetime."

"It was. You died on twenty-one June. Dead on the Evac helicopter. The PJs[5] that saved your life also ended it. They gave you more morphine on the bird, not knowing you'd already been pumped up pretty good. Your heart stopped. The PJs brought

---

5 PJ – Para-Rescue. Originally called Para-Jumper (PJ), these Air Force Special Operators are "Medics from the sky," known for their fearlessness in rescuing injured American military in combat. Motto: "That Others May Live."

you back. So, you were dead, then alive. You got a new birthday. Your Alive Day."

"My friends didn't get one of those," I said. It just came out, along with a new river of tears.

"Nope. And that truly sucks, my friend. You think that only happened to you?"

"Nah. I never asked you," I said quietly.

"Nope. Been waiting for the question.

"You mind talking about it?" I asked.

"Not any more or less than you do. It doesn't make me happy, but it doesn't cripple me every time anymore, either." He pointed to his prosthetic legs. "See what I did there?"

"You're hilarious," I said.

"I can talk about it. And you need to be able to talk about it. It gets easier, I promise."

"That's what everyone keeps telling me."

"Because it's true! Man, we lose so many vets to suicide every day. Every time I read about another one, I think, damn! If he'd just waited a little longer, he might have made it. You gotta *fight*, Sean!"

"I'm not going to kill myself. I'm glad I'm alive. I just … I just miss my friends. That's all."

"And that's normal. And so is feeling guilty. It's *normal*. Bottom line is, you and me—we're *here*, brother. We're here."

"Yeah. So what happened to you?"

"Foot patrol."

"I see what you did there," I said, chucking my chin at him.

"Now everybody's a comedian. We were in Khost, not too far from Camp Pucino. Foot patrol heads out to talk to some elders in a village that was helping the Muj ..."

"Didn't they *all* help the Muj?" I said with disdain.

"Pretty much. But these guys were bad at faking being friendly. What pissed me off was that we'd been there a few times. We built a well for these guys. Built a school for the region. Really tried to help these people. So how did they say thanks for the fresh water and school and supplies? They stored weapons and food for a company-sized element of foreign fighters. I was with a platoon of Rangers tasked with sneaking in and scoping out the village. We were just supposed to watch, and if we saw the Muj show up, we were going to paint it up with lasers and call in the heavy stuff.
"

"Roger that."

"Yeah, so, we get up into the mountains and we're moving around in the rocks, and bam—the Muj was all around us. Fuckers were in every cave and behind every rock and tree. We never saw them coming, like we were a bunch of new National Guardsmen or something. The fuckers were *good*, man. We're just quietly moving through the rocks, thinking we're invisible, and all of a sudden the RPGs hit us. Mortars come next, and then AK fire thick as hornets. They had us surrounded. We called in air support, and thank God some Warthogs were nearby. Somewhere in the middle of all this, my lieutenant, a guy named Hoskins, gets hit right in the face. I know he's dead, but I can't just leave him there, so I run over to grab him and pull him behind the rocks where I had been taking cover. An RPG landed right at my feet and that was it."

"Shit."

"Yeah. Shit. But Lieutenant Hoskins, he was a solid guy. Couldn't run and leave him there, you know? So I'm bleeding out and I reach for my tourniquet in my cargo pants' pocket, except it isn't there because I don't have my cargo pants because they must be on my legs a hundred yards away or some shit …"

"Been there, done that," I said, thinking back to lying in the dusty road.

"Yeah, well, Doc runs over in the middle of so many bullets you could almost *see* them, man. I don't even mean the tracers, I mean the fucking bullets! They were coming in like sleet. And fucking Doc runs straight through that shit to get to me."

"Corpsmen and medics. A different breed, that's for sure."

"So Doc Rozga runs to me and puts on tourniquets while covering me with his own body and saves my life. Then he grabs my M4 as I'm blacking out and pops two Hajis at almost point-blank range. They fell down almost on top of me, that's how close they were."

"Shit."

"Yeah, it was nuts, man. I felt so worthless. I mean, I was in shock and almost dead, but I still wanted a weapon. Still wanted to fight, you know? I wanted to help my guys. I figured I was dead anyway—I just wanted to take some hajis with me. At that moment I was more pissed than afraid or hurt. Then everything went black and I woke up here, same as you."

"When was that?"

"Three years ago."

"Your guys make it out okay?"

Darryl's eyes filled with water and his voice cracked. "I found out later on that Doc Rozga died in that fight. Never even got to thank the man."

It was heavy. "At least I got to thank Deke," I said.

"Yeah," he said, wiping his face. "So you keep working to get better. That feeling of guilt that we all walk around with deep inside—you gotta let it go."

"Did you?"

Darryl shrugged. "It's a work in progress, but yeah. I know I would have done anything to help my guys. Even my dead lieutenant. And they all did the same for me. And your friends did the same for you. It's how it is, man. We take care of each other."

I nodded, staring at my shoe that contained a fake foot.

Darryl continued. "I think back and I wonder. The LT, he was already dead. Was it worth losing both my legs to try and grab a guy that was already dead? I mean, I saw him get hit in the face. He was *gone*, man. But we don't leave each other out there like fucking chopped meat. Of *course* I had to get him. And Doc Rozga—he wouldn't leave me hanging in the breeze either. Charged through the bullets like he couldn't possibly be hurt." His voice cracked again. "Fuckin' Doc. He was a badass motherfucker, I tell you what." He looked up into the heavens and gathered himself, maybe talking to his friend.

He looked at me, the most serious expression I'd ever seen, and said, "So now I took care of you. And you're good to go, Sean. You go out into the world and figure out what it is you need to do, and make this second chance at being alive worthy of all the work and sacrifice."

"I owe you a lot," I said, feeling a little choked up myself.

"Damn straight. So make the effort worth it."

"Thanks, Darryl. I mean it."

"My pleasure, Sean. It truly was. First time I saw you, you were in a coma. Wasn't sure you'd even live. Then, a few days later, you were awake. Then you almost died again from that blood clot. You've had a rough few months, and I hate to remind you, but there may still be more shit down the road. Little surgeries here and there. They cut you and pull out some metal and then cut you again and remove some bone. And there's gonna be some days you want to quit. There's gonna be some days you're going to see the faces of your friends and you're going to forget why you're supposed to be alive when they aren't. And you *will* remind yourself that you're a Marine and you don't quit. *Ever*. And whether it's God's will, or dumb luck or fate or just how the universe spins, you're *here*, man. And you have a chance that your friends didn't get. So don't fuck it up."

"Rah." It was all I could think of to say.

Chapter 13
Liberation Day

I was in between sessions of physical therapy, getting ready to leave Walter Reed for good, when Deke showed up unannounced. I was almost asleep when I heard his familiar "Oooohhhh Rrraaaaaah …"

"Deke? What the hell are you doing here?"

"Babysitting, apparently."

I sat up in bed. "What day is it?" I asked.

"Twenty-one September. Time for you to get the hell out of here. There's a lot of seriously injured people in here that need that bed. You just had a little mishap, that's all. You need to Charlie-Mike, Nichols."

Charlie-Mike. Continue mission. "Yeah. I've been trying not to take any more drugs. Hurts like hell, but I hate feeling like a zombie and not being able to take a crap. I want to get out of here. I'm just not sure where I'm supposed to go."

Deke folded his arms. He knew my life story. He knew there was no family waiting out in the world somewhere to take me home and help me start a new life. It was just me, now, without my Marine Corps family.

"Well, Nichols, living here for the next seventy years isn't an option, so I think it's time you figured out where you want to be and ruck the fuck up."

"Did you talk to anyone? They say I'm being released?"

Deke motioned with his chin at the door. "They're coming now. I'm gonna split. Ain't supposed to be in here right now. I'll catch you later."

Deke left and five minutes later Dr. McGloughlin and a nurse entered my room.

"How's the patient?" asked the doc.

"Good. I'm good, Doc. Ready to get out of here."

"And that you shall!" he announced happily. "Today's the day. Lots of paperwork, and then you'll be formally discharged. Any idea of where you're going?"

"I have to make a few visits," I said. "Squid's little sister, Abby …" I found myself getting choked up.

The doctor leaned in real close and looked me in the eyes. "Sean, you're going to be fine physically. It takes a while, but you'll get used to your prosthetic and you'll do just fine. Mentally and emotionally, sometimes it's a little harder. I'm giving you a few phone numbers. You're never alone, Sean. You understand?"

"Yeah, I'm good, doc. Thanks for everything. You, too, Maureen. I mean it. When you weren't torturing me, you really helped a lot."

She gave me her raised-eyebrow look. "I can still order a catheter for you, mister."

"I'm *so* out of here."

"Show me," she said, crossing her arms.

I quickly stood up out of bed and walked around the small room. "Ta da!"

She balled up a piece of paper, threw it across the room and said "Fetch."

I quickly walked over, bent down, picked it up and jogged back to her like a dog, bowing and handing it to her with great drama. She smiled and surprised me with a hug. "Well done, sir. You'll be dancing in no time."

I danced her around the room for a quick second, which got smiles from her and Dr. McGloughlin.

"You're going to need lessons, and it has nothing to do with your leg," she said with a smile.

The doctor laughed. "Did we accidently give him two left feet?"

The nurse stepped away and gave me a real smile. "I'm proud of you, Sean. Now follow me and we'll get the paperwork started. By the time we're finished, I'll be moving you to the geriatric ward."

In true military fashion, the paperwork was overwhelming. Apparently, getting blown up required a lot of papers in triplicate. I'd also be getting a check once a month in the mail at some point for disability. Maybe I wouldn't end up homeless after all. After several hours of form-filling, and brief conversations and goodbyes with some of the other wounded folks I had met at Walter Reed, I was released. Just like that. See ya.

I walked outside in my USMC sweatsuit, feeling as ready as I could be, and watched happy reunions and families helping loved ones. I found myself smiling at the amount of palpable love I was witnessing. Suddenly, I felt very alone in the world. I took out one of my only worldly possessions, my cell phone, to call Deke. That's when I heard his very respectful greeting from a few yards away.

"Hey! Fucktard!"

As usual, Deke made me smile and feel better when I was feeling down.

"Hey man. I wasn't sure you were still around."

"I told you, I look after my peeps."

"You still have more time off?" I asked.

"I told you, I have as much time as you need. I didn't forget about our road trip."

I looked around at the tearful reunions and thought about Abby and my promise to Squid. "Yeah, we got to go see Abby."

"We need wheels. There's a car rental place around the corner. You got some cash?"

"Yeah, I'm loaded at the moment. Not sure how long it's gonna last before I have to get an actual j-o-b, but I'm good for a while."

"All right then, no excuses. *Road trip!*" He smacked me and smiled, and some of the weight and darkness left my chest. We started walking to the rental place.

"I don't know what I'd say to Abby. You'll have to do the talking."

Deke stopped walking, so I did, too. We faced each other and he got real serious. "No. Fucking. Way. Squid was your best friend, and the whole team knew Abby had a crush on you—including Squid. It's why he made you promise to go see his family if anything ever happened to him. This is coming from you, Marine." He poked my chest to punctuate his comments.

I started to speak with a "But ..."

"No buts! You'll figure it out. She's just gonna be happy to see you, man. And Frank's counting on you. Let's go. We need wheels."

"You gonna drive?" I asked.

He stopped again and cocked his head, looking like a pissed-off drill sergeant. "Look, Fucktard, I'm not here to be your babysitter. You're going to learn to drive with your left foot. My uncle drove a taxi, and he always drove with two feet. It ain't that hard driving with your left foot." He paused, then smirked. "You might not mention to the dude behind the counter you only have one leg, though. Might make him a little nervous."

Deke was either being a prick or was just trying to show me some "tough-love," but he wouldn't even come into the rental office with me. I was slightly terrified and did my best not to limp. My leg tends to squeak, and I was praying the guy wouldn't ask me any questions about it. In the end, I rented a car and walked out to find Deke smiling and shrugging with an "I told you so" look. I managed to back my ass into the car and sit down behind the wheel for the very first time. My prosthetic leg was in the way, so I picked it up and bent it across my lap in an anatomically impossible position. It may have looked ridiculous, but it was functional.

The first few minutes of driving was a cross between terrifying and hysterical. Deke found it very entertaining until I slammed the brakes so hard at a traffic light I launched us into the windshield.

"Relax, dude. You're doing fine. Just chill out. When we get on the highway, you can use cruise control. Just don't survive an IED, a hundred surgeries and an embolism so you can die in a car wreck."

"Funny to be on a road where there's no shit to blow you up, huh?" I asked.

"I'm not so sure. We passed like ten chicks texting and driving that almost crashed into us. If you weren't such a shitty driver, you'd have noticed."

"I told you, you can drive if you want."

"And I know you remember what I told *you*."

"Such a supportive friend. Thanks."

"I saved your ass once. That's all you get."

Damn. I felt my eyes get watery again. It was so random and embarrassing. I took a breath and said, "No, man. You saved my life when I got here, too. About fifty times." We drove in silence for a second. "There were a lot of days in that hospital I was ready to give up. The pain was so bad sometimes. The rehab sucked. And all the meds. Shit, man. If it wasn't for you, I don't know if I would have made it."

"Simmer down."

"I mean it, man. You see all those happy families outside the hospital? I don't have any family. Just you and the guys. And the *guys* are all *dead*. Where's my family now, Deke? Everyone's dead!" I started losing it again. Shit.

"Ruck up. Don't do that. Your brothers are always with you. Always. Now shut the fuck up and drive."

I managed to croak, "Yes, Sergeant."

We drove a long time listening to music, a little lost in our own thoughts. I had plugged the address into my phone's GPS to find Squid's family and just followed the map with Deke occasionally playing navigator. I'd actually been there before and had dinner with them. Squid lives in New York City. Lived. Lived in New York City.

"Squid's uncle was a New York City fireman. You know that?"

Deke grunted. "Yeah, I remember."

"All he wanted was some payback for his uncle on 9-11. Instead, his family got to bury another one of their own."

Deke took a deep breath and squeezed my shoulder. "Abby will be happy to see you, Sean. Seriously, you're doing the right thing. Squid's happy."

"You just talk to him or something?" I asked.

"Every day, bro."

Chapter 14
Squid's House

We drove around the Bronx neighborhood for quite a while, trying to find parking. Eventually, we got lucky and found a spot down the block from Squid's house.

"You shoulda got handicapped plates," Deke said as I parked.

"Fuck you."

I parked and looked at Sergeant Tilman. "Come on, this is gonna suck."

"This is all you, bro."

"What the fuck?" I shouted at him.

"Seriously. Squid was your bro. Abby will want alone-time with you. It's going to be hard, man."

"You're not even coming in?" I asked incredulously.

"Nah. Just along for the ride. Needed to make sure you didn't crash this nice new car. Not bad, by the way. The left-footed driving, I mean."

I was still staring at him in shock, feeling pissed. "You really aren't even coming in?"

"It's all you. Go."

"He was on your squad! What the fuck?"

"Go." He looked straight ahead and tuned me out.

"What if I'm in there for five hours?"

"Then I'll take a nap. Go see Abby."

I was so pissed I slammed the door extra hard when I got out; I had to force myself to calm down. I pulled my phone out and leaned against the car. My heart was pounding in my chest when I dialed his house.

A young familiar voice answered. "Hello?"

"Abby?"

"Yes?"

"Hey, Little Squid"

There was a slight pause, and she shouted, "*Sean?*"

"Yeah."

"Oh my God! *Sean!*" I could hear her start crying. "*Sean!*"

"I wanted to make sure you were home. Your parents home, too?"

"Yeah. They'll want to talk to you, too."

"Then open the front door. I'll be there in twenty seconds. 1477, right?"

"You're *here*?! Sean? *You're here?*"

I heard the phone hit the floor with a clunk, and then I could see Little Squid run out of her house down the block. She was sprinting down the block, bawling so hard I could hear her from six houses away. She ran into my arms so hard I almost went down, grabbing her a little too hard to keep from falling.

"Easy, Little Squid!" I said, trying to regain my balance. I had to readjust my leg, which she had almost knocked off, and she saw me do it. Her tears started flowing faster, with her hands now over her mouth.

"Sean? Oh my God! Sean?"

I forced a smile. "Yeah. I got a little dinged up."

She hugged me again so tight it almost hurt. And also felt so good I didn't want to let go. I could smell her hair conditioner, or whatever chicks use, and it smelled so good. A million miles away from the stench of Afghanistan. We hugged each other and cried, rocking back and forth for a very long time. As I blinked away tears, I could see Mr. and Mrs. Skidaro walking down the block towards us, concerned that their daughter had screamed and run out of the house. They broke into a jog when they saw it was me.

We ended up having a four-person hug-fest in the middle of the sidewalk. A few times I heard Mrs. Skidaro say she thought I was dead. There was a lot of hugging and crying going on. Eventually, we all regrouped, and Mrs. Skidaro took charge of the situation with Super-Mom-like abilities. She cleared her throat and grabbed my hand and ordered me to come home and eat. As she walked me quickly down the sidewalk, my limp became apparent. I'd been sitting for hours and was stiff. My gait was off, and the limp was obvious.

"You okay, son?" asked Mr. Skidaro, his face showing concern. I caught Abby shaking her head no at him, I guess trying to tell him not to ask.

"Yeah, thanks. It's getting better." I didn't know what to say really, so I just pulled the sweatpants' leg up enough to show them my new appendage. Mrs. Skidaro's hands flew to her face to cover her mouth and Mr. Skidaro's mouth just opened. I shrugged. "Yeah. I'll tell you everything when we sit down."

They both grabbed an arm, like I needed assistance. I didn't, but appreciated their concern and found it easier to just let them. We walked back to their house and up the steps into their home. I was greeted by a picture of Frank, in his dress blues, that punched me in the heart and literally took my breath away. I made myself breathe and keep walking.

We walked into the kitchen and sat at their table. Mrs. Skidaro was probably stressed out, and dealt with it by moving a hundred miles an hour. She was stirring sauce, grabbing plates and dishes, moving around like a line chef in a diner. Mr. Skidaro grabbed two beers out of the fridge and popped them both, putting one down in front of me. It was a little early in the day, but who was I to argue?

"You have such a nice house. It's great to see you all again," I said, feeling awkward.

Mrs. Skidaro was a few feet away, stirring something that smelled amazing. She stopped and looked at me with a forced smile. "Frankie grew up here. You can see his room if you want." That brought more tears, and Mr. Skidaro hopped up and walked over to hold her.

"Easy, Emma. We're so lucky to have Sean here."

She wiped her face quickly. "Of course. Sean. I'm sorry. We're so glad to see you. We didn't know what happened to you. We were so worried. Mrs. Adams called from Chicago. She told us about Charles. That's all we knew. It's good to see you, Sean. So good to see you."

She grabbed some silverware and set it down on the table. "Let me get you some food. You must be starving."

I thought about Deke missing this food back in the car. Fuck 'im. "I could eat. Haven't had real food in … I don't even know. I guess since Spade's mom, Mrs. Adams, I mean, sent us a package. Man, that was so many months ago."

"Why didn't you call to tell us you were all right? We thought you were dead, Sean," asked Mrs. Skidaro.

"I wasn't all right. It took a long time to get better. The first month I was so out of it. Surgery after surgery. It's been a long few months of rehab."

She smiled softly, like a mom looking at her baby. "I wouldn't have even noticed, Sean. You walk just fine."

"You really do, Sean. You look great," said Abby. She reached out and held my forearm with her hands, not letting go.

Mrs. Skidaro moved quickly about the kitchen and started putting together a plate of food. It was Chicken Parmesan that she started spooning tomato sauce over from the big pot on the stove. I could smell it from across the kitchen and my mouth literally watered. She walked back over and placed a huge plate of food in front of me, then shot Mr. Skidaro a look. "You'll eat later. Sean needs to eat." She shot Abby a look. "Get Sean a glass! And some bread! What are we, animals?"

I laughed. "Thank you, Mrs. Skidaro. It looks amazing. Aren't you all going to eat?"

"It's early for us, dear. But you need a good meal. We want to hear everything. After you eat. Please, *mangia, mangia*—eat."

I knew they wanted to know what happened to Frank. It's why I had driven almost five hours. But still, the food smelled too good. I had to eat first. It was a little awkward at first, eating while they just sat and watched, but after a few bites, I was so excited about the food I just cleaned my plate. I looked up and realized I had been eating like an animal. Mrs. Skidaro was beaming.

"You like my cooking?"

"Oh my God. Mrs. Skidaro, this is the best food I ever had in my life. I'm not being polite. It was amazing. I can't believe Frank didn't weight three hundred pounds."

Abby smiled at me and used a napkin to wipe the side of my mouth. "You should stay a while. Mom's an awesome cook."

Mr. Skidaro finished his beer and got up to bring two more. I had barely touched mine—too busy eating, but he didn't even notice. He put another beer in front of me with a slightly shaky hand. I think he knew the story was coming, and he wasn't quite ready for it. He took a very long slug of his beer before placing it down, clearing his throat, and saying, "So, Sean. Can you tell us about Frank?"

Mrs. Skidaro shot her husband a look, perhaps angry about him chugging beer number two. She quietly said, "Mrs. Adams called us about Charles. She asked us about Frankie. She didn't know."

"You didn't get a letter?" I asked.

"We did," interjected Mr. Skidaro. "And a visit from the Marine Corps. They were all very nice, but no one really knew anything."

"They just said the truck hit a land mine," said Mrs. Skidaro.

"An IED, Em," corrected her husband.

She looked at him coldly. "It blew up. That's all they said."

I took a deep breath and a swig of my beer, and nodded as I gathered my courage. "Okay. Mrs. Skidaro, come sit down. Everyone just sit and I'll try and tell you everything."

A quiet overtook the entire house that sucked the air out of the room.

"So they didn't tell you anything other than the truck hit an IED?" I asked.

"No. Just that our son was killed in southern Afghanistan, near the Pakistan border, by an IED. That's it," Mrs. Skidaro said. Her face had gone from motherly warmth to a dead void.

"That's right. Helmand Province. We were maybe thirty miles from the Pakistan border. A lot of weapons and foreign fighters come through that area."

Mrs. Skidaro reached out and took my hand. "Is this okay, Sean? I mean, do you mind talking about this?"

"Mrs. Skidaro, you're the first people I've talked to about anything, other than Deke and the people at the hospital. I drove here to tell you about what happened. I promised Squid I'd come see you. And Abby."

Abby squeezed my arm.

"So anyway, we were on patrol heading southeast towards the border and were going through a little village. There were five trucks. For whatever reason, Deke's truck, up front, rolled over the IED and nothing happened. We were in truck two, in a cruddy Humvee that none of us liked because it was old, with light armor, and had an air conditioner that never worked."

"Why light armor?" asked Mr. Skidaro, his face showing anger, I think.

"Because the good truck had gotten hit a few weeks before and was waiting for parts. They gave us a spare truck. So anyway, we were truck two, and we rolled over the IED. Sometimes they use pressure plates, and sometimes they use a phone to detonate them from somewhere where they can see us. All I know is, we hit a big one. Probably an EFP, an explosively formed projectile. They're wicked. Probably would have gone through even our Rhino. If it's any consolation, I know for a fact that Frank didn't suffer. He never knew what happened. One second we were driving, the next, I was in the road."

Mrs. Skidaro reached out and held Mr. Skidaro's hands in both of hers. Abby was still holding my forearm. The room seemed tiny.

"I was just lying on my back, and the lights were slowly coming back on, ya know? Then Deke, our sergeant, comes charging through the bullets like Superman. He grabs me by my vest and pulls me out of the road, firing his weapon at the Hajis and screaming commands at the guys. I couldn't really hear him. I just saw him. Then I saw my leg."

"Oh, Sean, it must have hurt so bad," said Abby.

"No. That's the thing, Abby. At first, I didn't feel *anything*. Doc said that happens sometimes when you're in shock. I just saw my leg bone sticking out. Sorry. Didn't mean to be gross. But, I saw it, ya know? Then Deke pulls me behind this wall and he's just laying it down at the Muj like a madman. The corpsman comes up and pops a morphine syringe into me just as it's starting to hurt, and I kind of blacked out, I guess."

"So Frank was still in the truck?" asked Mr. Skidaro.

"Sorry. Well. Um. He and Spade—that's what we call Chuck. I mean Charles. Charles Adams was Chuckie Spade to us. Like Frank was Squid." I looked at Abby, who looked so sad. "Like you're Little Squid." I gave her hand a little squeeze. "See, there was four of us in the Humvee. Sorry, I should have said that. Squid was driving. Your son, Frank. He was driving. And Spade was riding shotgun. Except he never carried a shotgun, he was our machine-gunner. Big machine gun. He was lethal. Chuckie Spade." I felt my voice crack when I said his name. I don't know why that happens sometimes.

The faucet just came on again. I wanted to punch Deke for not coming in at that moment.

"You're doing fine, son," said Mr. Skidaro. He chugged his beer and got up to grab two more, ignoring his wife's angry face. My second beer was untouched. He came back with two more and put the new full one next to the other full one.

When he was seated, I continued. "Sorry. Squid driving. Spade up front. Mack and me in the back. Mack—that's Johnny MacNamara. We call him Mack. Or Johnny Mack. *Called* him. Called him Johnny Mack. When we got hit, I was blown out of the truck. 'Cause it was so hot. I had opened the door a little to get some air, see? Next thing I know—I'm just lying in the road. Someone was nearby. I'm guessing it was Mack, because he was next to me in the back. The front got hit worse. I think, no, I know, that Frank and Spade were killed instantly. They didn't feel any pain. I promise."

I took a pause to sip my beer and wash down the lump in my throat. All three of them were wiping tears away. I drained the can.

"Did they burn in the truck?" asked Mr. Skidaro bluntly.

"Frank!" His wife looked appalled.

"I just want to know. They wouldn't let us see his remains. Said 'remains not suitable for viewing.'"

Mrs. Skidaro was now sobbing. "What does it *matter*? He was killed instantly! Isn't that right, Sean? He never felt anything ..."

"Yes, ma'am. I know he never felt anything."

Mr. Skidaro locked eyes with me and stared, waiting.

"Mr. Skidaro, the explosion was huge. It split the truck in two. That's how me and Mack ended up in the road, I think. Your son

… *my best friend* … and Spade … were still in the truck. I'm sorry. There was nothing I could do. Deke pulled me out of the road. I'd trade places with him, I swear to God!" Now I was crying, too. Shit. I promised myself I'd keep my shit together.

Mr. and Mrs. Skidaro both grabbed my hands and started saying, "No, no …" Abby was sobbing, her face in her hands. It was a shit-show.

I tried to comfort Mr. Skidaro. "The truck didn't really burn long. It was just a huge explosion."

Abby looked at me with huge, watery eyes. "He was already gone, though?"

"Yeah. One hundred percent, Abby. They were gone instantly."

"So your other friend Johnny Mack was killed as well?"

"I was the only one that made it out," I managed to say. The *"Why me?"* was unintentional, as was my sobbing. My attempt at getting through the story without making a scene ended in failure. I hid my face in my hands and bawled like a baby. Next thing I knew Mrs. Skidaro was up and around the table, hugging me. I just hung onto her, wrapped my arms around her middle, buried my face in her stomach and cried and cried until I could finally get my shit together. Abby was hugging me from the other side, crying as hard as I was. In my head, I apologized to Frank for fucking this all up.

After a minute or so, I had managed to control myself and apologize for losing control. Mrs. Skidaro had her hands on shoulders and looked me right in the eyes. She made a stern face and said, "Frank would be happy you're alive, Sean."

Abby added, "It's not your fault, Sean. I know Frank would be happy to know you made it."

I wiped my face and took a long chug of beer number two. Mr. Skidaro crushed his empty number three and walked to get a fourth, his eyes now glassy and far away. We all sort of just watched him go back and forth silently. He sat down and looked at me. "What happened after the truck was hit?"

"Deke pulled me out of the road and saved me, and then the Muj threw everything they had at us. RPGs, machine guns—it was chaos. Then I passed out. When I woke up, I was in a helicopter. Then they gave me more morphine, and I died. OD'd right there. Then the PJs—that's the para-rescue guys, they brought me back again, even though I don't remember any of that. Then I woke up again in a field hospital, I think, with other injured guys. Then next thing I knew I was in Walter Reed. No idea how I got there. I was pretty fucked up … sorry … I was banged up, ya know? Lots of pain meds." I had dropped the F-bomb in front of Mrs. Skidaro. Oops.

They all ignored it. Mr. Skidaro asked, "I thought PJs were Air Force?"

"Yes, sir. They just happened to be the closest support when we got hit to evacuate our dead and wounded. Those guys are crazy brave. I mean, we were ambushed and taking fire from everywhere, and these guys just roar in on helicopters and jump down into the mess. Anyway, they sorta killed me by accident, then brought me back on the bird. Took me to a field hospital somewhere, then I ended up at Walter Reed. Honestly, it's mostly just a blur. I only remember little bits and pieces."

"How long were you there? Walter Reed, I mean," asked Mr. Skidaro.

"Since twenty-three June, I guess. I just got out. Three months of surgeries, rehab, fittings for my leg. Not my best summer. Then I came right here, first stop." I looked at Abby, who was smiling at that information. "I promised Squid I'd come see you, Abby. I promised."

Abby squeezed my arm. "Thanks for coming, Sean. And I'm sorry about ... you getting hurt. Does it hurt bad?"

"Sometimes. It's weird. My *foot* hurts. I mean, obviously it isn't there. My brain doesn't seem to know it yet."

Mrs. Skidaro looked flustered. "It'll get better. Let me get you something else to eat." She started to get up, but I grabbed her hand and made her sit.

"No, no. Thank you. It was amazing. Best food ever. Seriously."

Mr. Skidaro had gotten quiet. I caught him staring at Frank's picture out in the hallway. He looked at me and just blurted, "Would you like to stay a few days? You're welcome to stay as long as you want."

"Thanks, but I can't ..."

"*Please?*" pleaded Abby. "Just stay a few days?"

"Sorry, Little Squid. I have to go see Mack's family. Maybe one day I'll get to Spade's, too, out in Chicago. But Johnny Mack lives in New Jersey. His family, I mean. Gonna go see his family, then go to Arlington and see them all." It was hard to say without that lump in my throat coming back.

"Frankie is in Arlington," said Abby. "We went in June." She paused and then started tearing up. She whispered, "I kept looking for your name as I walked through the rows."

I nodded. "Yeah. Mack and Spade are there, too. Deke and I are going to go visit them."

"Can I go with you?" asked Abby.

"Not this time. One day you'll take a ride down with me, okay?"

"Okay."

It was that awkward moment where I knew I had to go, but I didn't want another crying scene. I set my jaw and said, "It was nice to see you all again. I'm sorry about everything. Thank you so much for dinner."

Mrs. Skidaro stood up. "Sean, you take of yourself, and please stay in touch, okay? If you ever need anything, you call us?"

"Yes, ma'am."

"I mean it, Sean. Anything at all. You just call. Frank loved you, Sean. He'd be happy to know you made it."

"Thank you, Mrs. Skidaro. That means a lot. I loved him, too."

Mr. Skidaro looked a little wasted. "Sure you won't stay for another beer?" he asked. "You can stay over." He was staring at Frank's picture again.

"Thanks, Mr. Skidaro. I got to get back on the road. Deke and I need to see Mack's folks." We all exchanged hugs and back-pats and said goodbye. Abby cried again, but I told her I'd call her real soon. We could Skype again. That made her smile. Cute kid.

I walked out after brief hugs, trying not to look at Mr. Skidaro staring at Squid's picture.

Chapter 15
Road Trip

The walk back to my car seemed to take an hour. They wanted to walk me, but I insisted I was okay on my own. I needed to clear my head. Abby cried again as I hugged her at the door, and it broke my heart. She loved Squid so much. Her crush on me was just an extension of her brother's life that was now gone.

When I got to the car, Deke was sitting in the exact same position as when I'd left. Staring straight ahead like he was at "seated attention." I backed into the seat and adjusted the leg across my lap again, dropping my head back against the rest.

"Fuckin' brutal, man. His parents. Abby. They're all so sad."

"You okay?"

"Yeah. I just don't get it though, man. Why am I alive and everyone else is dead? Four guys in the same truck. One guy makes it out and three don't. What the fuck, man?"

"Some guys would say it's because God has a plan for you."

I looked over at him. I kinda wanted to smash his face in. "Seriously?"

Deke shrugged. "Some people believe that stuff. What about you? You believe it?"

"I don't know what I believe. I just know a year ago I had my leg and my best friends. The Corps is my family, Deke. You're all I got left. That's it. Just you."

"And I told you, I got your back. It's going to be too late to get to Johnny Mack's. We can't show up at ten and just knock on their door. Maybe drive to Jersey, find a hotel near a bar and get shit-faced."

"Yeah. I'd been to Squid's house before. Met his family. Never met Mack's folks. You?"

"Nope."

"Okay. So we head south to Jersey. Find a motel and have a beer or a hundred."

Deke nodded. "Roger that."

***

We got off the Turnpike in Jersey City and found a cheap motel right across the street from a dumpy-looking bar. We walked in and found a tiny table in the back of the dark bar. I think the floors had last been cleaned prior to my deployment. There were some pool tables and quite a few folks sitting at the bar and tables. I saw lots of Bud tall-necks and shots of Jack being carried around. Damn. I hadn't been in a bar in a long time. It's hard to describe what was in my head. I looked at Deke, so happy to see him and be in an American bar, with loud music I'd heard before and beer and whiskey. But Mack and Spade and Squid should have been with us, and it made my heart hurt. I sat back in the wooden chair and just took it all in.

A cute little waitress came by and I ordered us two beers and two shots of Jack. We were on a mission. A little while later, the collection of beer bottles and shot glasses had grown to an impressive pile. I just stayed in the chair, enjoying the feeling of being wasted on something other than morphine. I had closed my eyes without realizing it, singing along with the music, when Deke stood up and told me he was going to hit the head. I slurred a "Roger!"

A cute girl walked over as he left and put her hands on the table, leaning way over so I could see down her low-cut top. I couldn't even remember the last time I saw a real pair of tits. She looked at me and smiled and asked me, "Who's Roger?"

"Huh?"

"You were calling for Roger."

"No, I was talking to Deke."

She looked around, but Deke was already in the bathroom. She saw the four bottles and four shot glasses. "Is Deke your girlfriend?" she asked.

"Deke? He's my sergeant!"

"Uh-huh. A Marine?" she asked, her finger tracing the USMC on my chest. "I bet you look so handsome in your uniform."

I don't know why I did it. I picked up my right leg and laid it across my left like I was driving the car. The impossible angle of my foot made her jump back.

"What the fuck, man?"

"Oh. Yeah. That. Uniform probably fits funny now."

"Have fun with your boyfriend," She said. She walked away, looking pissed.

Deke walked right back past her and sat down. "What's up?" he asked.

"Ah, nothing. Some bimbo didn't like how my leg bends."

Deke looked at the ridiculous position of my leg. "You know, eventually you're going to need to get laid. You better learn to act like a normal guy who's just got a hitch in his giddy-up."

"Whatever."

"Hey man. You still got your junk. Be thankful of that. I mean, I assume you do, right?"

"My junk is just fine, thank you."

I flashed back to lying by the stone wall, bleeding out while Deke stood over me, returning fire. I remember being so relieved when I grabbed my junk and it was still there.

"Okay. So. You better learn not to be such an asshole."

"Your advice on women is hereby noted."

"Dude. You're a wounded warrior. Should make it easier to get laid, not harder. Work the Marine hero angle."

I felt the tears come back and leaned across the table. "I'm not a hero. I just lived and everybody else died. That's all that happened."

I chugged my beer and slammed it down on the table, way too hard. The bartender looked at me and yelled to his waitress. I saw them talking about me. He asked her if my tab was paid and she said yes. He came around the bar and walked up to us and said, "That's it, you're done. Goodnight."

When I stood up, I stumbled a little bit.

"You can't even walk. You're outta here!" he snapped at me.

I pulled up my sweatpants' leg and showed him my prosthetic. "Is that anything to say to a United States Marine with one leg? You go *fuck* yourself. Come on, Deke. Fuck these guys."

The bartender's face fell when he saw my leg. "You get home safe," he mumbled, then slinked back behind the bar.

Chapter 16
On The Road Again

It was an ugly morning. I woke up on a funky tiled floor next to a very old toilet bowl. My first instinct to stand up was met with a "Whoa, take it easy," from Deke, who was sitting on the edge of the bathtub in boxers. Yeah. Hard to jump up when one of your legs is across the room on the bed.

I rolled over and sat up. All I had on was my underwear. "Shit. Did I puke?"

"Yup. *You* are out of practice, my man. You used to be able to drink twice that much and not puke like some ninth grader."

I spit into the bowl and used the sink to pull myself up on one leg. I rinsed out my mouth and splashed water on my face. I felt like shit. I looked at Deke, who made zero effort to help me, and hopped my hungover-ass to the bed where I flopped down and rolled over.

After another hour of slow death, Deke yelled at me to get my ass up. I hopped back to the shower and had my first experience in a shower that didn't have ADA handrails for us handicapped types. I managed not to break my neck, but it was interesting. My duffel bag offered very little in the way of fashion. The Marine Corps had been kind enough to send my personal belongings in my duffel bag to Walter Reed, but it didn't have a whole lot in it that wasn't designed for combat. I settled for a pair of jeans and a USMC T-shirt in desert tan.

Once I was all cleaned up and feeling half-human, Deke looked at me and said, "You still look like shit."

"Thanks, Sergeant."

"That chick was totally diggin' you, man."

"Until she saw my leg."

"No, man. Until you acted like an asshole. You talk to a girl first. See if you like each other. If it's going well, she'll eventually figure it out. If she can't deal with it, then oh well. But you don't just whip out your leg in some ridiculous angle and try and scare her away."

"Whatever," I mumbled as I packed up the rest of my stuff to head out.

"Yo, man. You better stop feeling sorry for yourself or I'll shove that leg up your ass."

"Is that any way to treat a Marine hero?" I asked him.

"Fuck you. You just lived and everyone else died. That's all you did."

"Damn, man. That's cold."

"That's what you said last night."

Yeah, I guess I did. "I was wasted."

"Well obviously you were thinking it."

"Maybe."

"Yeah, well *un*-think it. You're alive. For whatever reason. You need to figure out what that reason is and do something with your second chance. Fifty years ago, you would have died on the battlefield. Now you're alive and you can walk just fine. Quit the guilty-depressed-self-pity-bullshit. *Ruck up, Marine.*"

We headed out to the car after a brief walk over to a neighboring shop for coffee. I plugged Mack's address into my phone GPS and started driving through Jersey City. Deke asked me, "You ever meets Mack's folks before?"

"No."

"What are you going to say to them?" he asked.

"I ain't sayin' shit," I said. "I did all the talking *last* time. *You're* the sergeant. You can talk this time."

We drove in silence for a moment.

"They were your fire team, in your truck. It's your deal, Corporal," said Deke quietly.

I was pissed. "For such a battle-hardened super hero, you sure are a pussy when it comes to talking to people."

"I only talk to you. That's it. I did enough screaming as a sergeant to last me a lifetime. I'm done talking to everyone else. I get to rest and relax and take it easy now."

"Seriously, man. You have to at least come in this time."

"We'll see. You've got another twenty minutes or so. Put on some good tunes and shut your pie hole."

We drove without speaking for most of the trip. The coffee helped me recover, and by the time I found a place to park on Kensington Avenue, I felt fairly normal. It was a tree-lined street of small, neat homes on postage-stamp-sized lots. I couldn't help but think the place looked like it probably hadn't changed a bit in sixty years.

When I killed the engine, I felt the dread of facing Mack's family. "I didn't have a phone number," I told Deke.

"Might not even be home," he said.

"You coming this time?"

"I told you, I'm done talking to people."

I stared at him, pissed off, but he looked a million miles away—just staring sadly straight ahead at absolutely nothing. I got out of the car and double-checked the address. It was a short walk to a small tidy house with giant elm trees out front. I walked up the porch and rang the bell, where I was greeted by a cautious face at the door.

"Mrs. MacNamara? I'm Sean Nichols. I served with …"

The door opened wide and Mrs. MacNamara stepped out and hugged me, saying, "I know exactly who you are! Johnny told us all about you!"

She started crying a little and called for her husband, who appeared in slacks and a rumpled shirt, the tie loose around his neck. A badge and holstered gun were on his belt. Mr. MacNamara was a Jersey City cop, and he looked exhausted.

Mrs. MacNamara started talking a hundred miles an hour. "Jimmy! This is Sean! Sean Nichols! One of Johnny's friends!"

Mr. MacNamara forced a polite smile and held the door open wide. "Nice to meet you, Sean. Come on in. I just got home. Worked midnights this week."

I smiled and walked into their house, which was orderly and clean like a Marine Corps barracks. Mr. MacNamara, ever the detective, noticed my limp.

"You get hurt over there, Sean?"

"Yes, sir."

"I'm sure it'll get better. Just a little limp. Barely noticeable," he said with that same forced smile.

I pulled up my jeans enough to show him my stick-for-a-leg. "Probably won't get much better than this. But I'm walking better than I was."

Mr. and Mrs. MacNamara both looked shocked and started talking a hundred miles an hour again, both apologetic and horrified.

"It's okay," I said.

"Can I get you some coffee?" asked Mrs. MacNamara.

"Sure, that'd be great," I replied and followed the two of them back into the kitchen. Their house wasn't much different than Squid's. We all stood there awkwardly while Mrs. MacNamara made coffee.

"It's nice to meet you in person," said Mr. MacNamara. "John told us that you were always looking out for him." That forced smile again. The man looked way older than he should.

I tried to find something to say. "I wish I could have looked out for him on twenty-one June."

"Were you there?"

"Yes, sir."

Mr. MacNamara nodded and took a long, slow breath. All of a sudden, my appearance meant the untold story of their son's death. Mr. MacNamara took his wife's arm and repeated the information to her. "Heather, Sean was with John when he was killed."

She poured three mugs of coffee and handed them out to us, then motioned towards the table. I wondered if the kitchen table was where all horrible news got delivered. We walked in and sat together.

"Is that when you got hurt?" asked Mack's mom, now looking very beaten like her husband.

95

"Yes, ma'am," I replied. I sipped my coffee and stared at the black liquid to avoid looking at them.

"Did you come to tell us about what happened? They didn't tell us much, you know," said Mrs. MacNamara.

"If you'd like to know, I can tell you. I came by, I don't know. I went and saw Squid's family—that's Frank Skidaro—he was on our fire team, too. Then, I don't know … I just thought I should come see you, too."

"Thank you, Sean. It's nice that you came by," said Mr. MacNamara. I wished he would quit smiling and trying to look happy. It wasn't working for him.

"Yes, thank you. Not knowing what happened that day has made it worse," said Mrs. MacNamara.

"Yes, I understand. I want you to know first off that John never felt any pain. It was instant."

"They told us it was an IED," said Mr. MacNamara softly.

"Yes, sir. That whole country is one big land mine. We were in a convoy heading out on a mission and our truck rolled over it. Johnny and Squid and Spade and me were all together in the truck. Johnny was sitting next to me in the back."

When I reached for the coffee to try and stay composed, my hand was shaking. I saw him clearly for the first time. Mack. In the road near me, blackened and smoldering. The whites of his eyes against his black face. Like he was staring right at me through his own smoke. I felt a shiver pass through me and almost dropped the mug.

"We were just driving. I cracked my door open a little because we were roasting in there. One second we're talking, and the next, I'm lying in the road without my leg and all Hell is breaking lose. Firefight's going on all around me. It happened in a split second.

I was the only one that made it out of the truck. Chuckie Spade, Squid, and your son John all died. And for no reason at all, I'm still here."

I took a sip of coffee and stared into the mug, trying not to look at his parents. The tears started coming again, which pissed me off.

Mr. MacNamara nodded and spoke quietly, "There's a reason. One day you'll know what it is. I know I'm glad to see you, Sean."

Mrs. MacNamara quietly cleared her throat and said, "It was the day before his birthday, did you know that?"

"Yeah. We had a little party the night before. I mean, nothing big. We didn't even have candles. But me and Squid got some candy and stuff and sang to him. We were gonna try and find some booze for him the next night. Pretty hard to get booze in Afghanistan. But we talked about it, ya know? We were gonna try and have a party."

We were all quietly wiping tears, avoiding eye contact. Everyone's voice had gotten very soft as we all struggled to speak. "So he had a little party, then?" asked his mom.

"Yes, ma'am. We all sang. It was pretty horrible singing."

"That's so nice. He had a little birthday party, Jimmy," she said, rubbing her husband's hand. Mr. Mack managed to nod, but let out a small yelp and wiped his face.

Mrs. MacNamara spoke so quietly I could hardly hear her, tears running freely down her cheeks. "He was such a good boy."

"Yes, ma'am. We all loved him. Johnny Mack. That's what we called him. It was his first tour and we looked out for him as best we could. I'm sorry I couldn't get him home." The apology came out as a messy wail. We all grabbed for each other's hands and just sat there with bowed heads, quietly crying at his kitchen table.

We stayed like that for a long time. Eventually, Mrs. MacNamara broke the spell because she had to blow her nose and wipe her face. We all grabbed our napkins and spent a few seconds honking and wiping and sort of laughing at each other, we were all such a mess.

"I'm sorry," I finally blurted. "I'm sorry. I was the NCO responsible for his safety. I never even had a chance to try and help him. I'm so sorry."

Mr. MacNamara smacked my hand a couple of times. "It's war, son. Good people die." He looked right through my eyes into my soul. "Good people get *hurt*, Sean. We don't blame you. We're not angry that you're alive and he isn't. We're glad you alive. And I hope you use this second chance to do something amazing. I know Johnny would want that for you."

There was more hugging and crying and some babbling, about what I can't recall. Then we said goodbyes, exchanged more hugs and promises of staying in touch, and I left.

As I walked out into the bright sunshine, I was surprised that it was daylight and beautiful outside. The inside of that house felt like death and darkness. Stepping outside was a reminder that I had an Alive Day. A second chance that Mack didn't get. I caught my breath and walked back to the car. I'm pretty sure they watched me walk all the way down the street, but I didn't turn around. They were looking at me, alive, and felt just a teeny bit closer to Mack because of our connection. I understood. I let them have their moment and just kept walking, doing my very best not to limp.

When I got back into the car, Deke was sitting stiffly again, staring straight ahead. When I slammed my door closed he asked, "You okay?"

"Fuck you."

"He was your friend."

"He was on *your* squad!" I shouted, a little louder than I meant.

"You needed to do it. And you know why."

I held the wheel and stared straight ahead.

Deke wouldn't let it go. "Tell me why," he said.

"Thanks for nothing," I muttered.

"Tell me why, Sean. Why did you need to go and not me?"

I started the car, but Deke put his hand on the wheel.

"Wait. Tell me. Why is it that I wanted you to go alone?" he said softly.

"I don't know!"

"Yes, you do," he said. "You still feel so guilty, Nicky. Why? I mean, it's okay to feel sad. To be lonely. I get it. But guilt? No way, man. You didn't do anything wrong. You were a good leader. A good Marine. I'd share a foxhole with you any day. But you're alive, Nicky. For whatever reason. And yeah, you got hurt and life isn't the same anymore. But you have a life, man. You have to live it. You owe it to the other guys."

"You done now?"

"Sure. But you think about it. Survivor's guilt is bullshit, man. It'll waste you. And there's no reason to let that happen."

"Everyone's dead!"

"Not everyone. We're sitting right here having a conversation. You need to think about what you can do to make things as right as you can. Making this trip was a good start."

"So now what? We have to drive all the way to Chicago?"

"One day. But I think we need to go to Arlington. It's maybe four hours from here. We can be there by three o'clock."

I felt a wave of sorrow wash over me. "It's going to be a really hard goodbye. I don't know if I can do it."

"The goodbye *already happened*. What has to happen next is making peace with it."

"I don't know if I can," I replied. It was getting hard to talk again.

"Then the wrong guy lived," said Deke so matter-of-factly the sword cut through my

chest.

"You're fuckin' relentless."

"No, man. I'm your friend. Your sergeant. And I saved your life for a reason. Don't you

ever forget that!"

"Everyone is *dead*, Deke!"

The tears were flowing again, and I wiped my nose on my arm.

Deke looked disgusted with me and shook his head. "Drive."

Chapter 17
Arlington National Cemetery

Section 60 was immaculate, like the rest of Arlington. Somewhere, further up the hill, a guard strode silent watch over the tombs of the unknown. Twenty-one steps, back and forth, in silent honors. Twenty-four-seven, three-sixty-five, in all weather. A guard would stand watch over the Gardens of Stone forever.

We had put on our Dress Blues and took the time to make sure our uniforms were perfect. My brass was polished and unmarred, and there wasn't a speck of lint on anything. Deke and I looked at each other and tightened our jaws, gave each other a quick nod, and put on our covers, pulled down low. I hadn't worn my Dress Blues in maybe a year. Putting them on reminded me that I was still a United States Marine, and would be until my last breath.

I checked the piece of paper again and double-checked the locations of where our friends were buried. Section 60 was the permanent home to my fire team, as well as many other brothers and sisters who had given their final measure in Afghanistan and Iraq. Deke and I walked in silence to find Squid's marker. Truth be told, we didn't walk, we *marched*, as perfectly as we knew how. We marched slowly, eye-balling each marker until we found our friend.

Deke and I stopped and stood over Squid's marker. Like the others, it was white. Elegant in its simplicity. A small cross was carved above his name.

FRANK SKIDARO
LCPL USMC
AFGHANISTAN
PURPLE HEART
12-1-1992
6-21-2014

We just stood there staring for a while.

"Shoulda said 'Squid' on there," I said quietly.

Deke shrugged. "The ones who matter know."

That made me remember an old saying, modified from Saint Thomas Aquinas. *For the ones that have been there, no explanation is necessary. For the ones that haven't, no explanation is possible.*

Deke used a very quiet sergeant growl to command "*Attennnnnn-tion.*" We snapped to attention as if we were on a parade ground. Deke whispered, "*Hannnnnd Salute,*" and we snapped a salute to the Squid Man. We held it there for a long time, and then brought it back down very slowly. My chest hurt.

"I saw Abby and your folks, Squid. Just like I promised." I whispered. "They're gonna be okay. Need some more time, ya know? Little Squid is growing up, man. I'll bring her back here one day to visit you, I promise. And I'll check in on her from time to time. We miss you, brother."

"Come on," said Deke.

We walked in silence through the grass to our next destination. There was no air in Arlington. It was just a vacuum. My collar felt tight. Chuckie Spade wasn't so far from Squid, which made me happy. They'd rest together for eternity.

Standing over the white marker, we looked down to see our friend.

CHARLES ADAMS
CPL USMC
AFGHANISTAN
PURPLE HEART
8-12-1991
6-21-2014

Deke ordered attention again, and we repeated the honor guard salute, slowly and with purpose.

"Spade," I said quietly. My voice cracked a little. "A one-man wrecking crew. One hundred percent badass. Chuckie. You sure sent a lot of Dirt Merchants ahead of you. Damn fine Marine. Semper Fi, bro."

Deke whispered, *"Ooohh Rah."*

Walking to Johnny Mack seemed to take forever. My legs weighed a thousand pounds—even the titanium one. I fought the spasms in my chest and snapped to attention with Deke as I looked down on the perfect white stone.

JOHN MACNAMARA
LCPL USMC
AFGHANISTAN

PURPLE HEART
6-22-1994
6-21-2014

Day before his birthday. Shit. I was having trouble seeing the marker and kept blinking the water out of my eyes.

"Didn't even make twenty," I said to Deke. "That's fucked up."

"The Suck don't care how old you are," said Deke.

"Sorry, Johnny Mack. You were going to be a great Marine. Didn't even finish your first tour. Least you had some candy, right? Sorry about the bottle of Jack. Squid and I planned that for weeks." My voice cracked and I took a second to collect myself. "They had a big parade for you in Jersey City. I hope you saw it from up there. You woulda liked it. We saw your mom and dad. They're good folks. They miss you, bro. Me, too."

We just stood there staring at the white marble for a while.

"We have one more to visit," said Deke.

"I can't. I'm done, man. It's too much."

"We have to. It's close. Come on, brother. You know you have to come with me."

The tears started flowing. Mr. Tough Guy Marine. I couldn't turn off the faucet. "Come on, man. Another day, okay?"

Deke shook his head sadly, then growled his sergeant voice again, "Suck it up, Marine. Get your gimpy ass movin'." He turned and started walking, and I walked after him as fast as I could to keep up. It was a further walk than it had been from Chuck to Squid to Mack. Going up a hill in the grass made my limp obvious.

"Slow down, man," I said.

Deke ignored me and chugged along, in case I was going to try and talk him out of going again.

We walked and walked, up that hill. My legs grew heavier with each step. My fake leg hurt and squeaked, and I swung it out to the side a bit with each step as I forced my hips to keep up. Deke finally stopped and I stood next to him.

"*Please* don't fuck this up, Marine," he said quietly, closing his eyes.

We snapped the salute and held it there. My eyes were on the marker, but it was impossible to read the letters through my tears.

DEACON TILMAN
SGT USMC
IRAQ
AFGHANISTAN
SILVER STAR
2-20-1990
6-21-2014

I held it for a long time. Seemed like I would hold it there forever. Seconds became minutes. My arm started to cramp. I'm not sure how long I stood there. I finally brought it down slowly. So slowly.

"Deke," I whispered hoarsely through the tears. "Deke. You shoulda left me in the road, man. You coulda taken cover and you'd still be here. Fucking John Wayne."

Arlington had never been quieter. Just the leaves gently rustling in the warm breeze. Birds singing reminded me I was alive. I looked up into the sun and felt the warmth on my face.

I was alive.

Because of Deke.

"Deke?" I looked over and he was gone. "Deke!" I screamed so loud it echoed through the cemetery. "Come back! I need you!"

I sat in the perfectly manicured grass and let it all out. There was a lot that needed to come out.

It took a while to get back up. But it had to be done perfectly. I owed Deke that much. I snapped to attention so hard I could feel every muscle in my body harden into steel. I set my jaw and showed Deke my War Face.

"Sergeant Deacon Tilman, United States Marine Corps!" I bellowed. My voice echoed for only an instant, then disappeared into the void of Arlington.

Epilogue

I was running as hard as I could, the sweat pouring down my face. My gray USMC sweatshirt was dark and soaked.

"Let's go, Marine!" I screamed. "You got this!"

"It hurts, man!" shouted Gary. He was twenty years old, running on a fake leg, just like me. He was also missing his right eye and had severe burn scars all over his face.

"Ruck up! Finish strong! People are watching—you're a *Marine!*"

The two of us crossed the imaginary finish line almost together and broke stride, slowing down until we stopped, hands on our thighs, almost doubled over in agony. We coughed and laughed as we tried to control our breathing.

"Thirteen minutes? Are you *shittin'* me?" bellowed Darryl, staring at his stop watch. "My mother runs *two* miles in thirteen minutes!"

"Your mother has *two legs!*" I shouted back at him.

"And they're bowlegged!" he replied, his face breaking into his huge toothy grin. He walked towards us with Nicole, the nurse on the third floor I'd been spending some time with lately. Her smile reached all the way into my chest and reminded my heart it did more than pump blood.

I smacked Gary on his shoulder. "Good work, Dog. We're getting there."

"I didn't think I was gonna make it," he said between ragged breaths.

"But you did. Just like me. We're gonna make it, bro. One day at a time. We're gonna make it."

***

Thank You, Veterans. This one was just for you.

ABOUT THE AUTHOR

David M. Salkin has been writing novels since 2005. His collection continues to grow, with the ultimate goal of seeing his books on the Big Screen. The screenplay version of BATTLE SCARS is what prompted the writing of this novella.

David has served Freehold Township, NJ since 1994 in many capacities, including Mayor, Deputy Mayor, Township Committeeman and Police Commissioner. He's also an associate member of the Philip A. Reynolds Detachment of the Marine Corps League, where he gets to work alongside real heroes. Dave also serves as a board member of the Veterans Community Alliance – Freehold Township Day Committee. The VCA has helped local veterans and given out more than $100,000 to assist those veterans and their families.

When not working, Dave prefers to be under the waves, Scuba diving with his family; or, depending on the season, screaming at his favorite team, the football Giants. An avid chef and wine aficionado, Dave has perfected many recipes in the parking lot of Giants Stadium over the years.

Be sure to visit **DavidMSalkin.com** for the latest news on new releases, appearances & book signings, bad jokes and stream of consciousness musings. Heck, he may even post a recipe in there with his favorite wine pairing…there's just no way to guess.

You can also become a fan on Facebook, (Author David M. Salkin) or follow Dave on twitter @DavidMSalkin.

The David M. Salkin Collection

Military Espionage / Action-Adventure
The Team (Series published by Post Hill Press)
The Team II – Into the Jungle
The Team III – African Dragon
The Team IV – Shadow of Death
The MOP
The Team V – Dangerous Ground
Crescent Fire (Penguin Books)
Necessary Extremes (Penguin Books)

Crime Thrillers
Hard Carbon (Post Hill Press)
Deep Down

Science-Fiction / Horror / Action-Adventure
Deep Black Sea (Permuted Press)
Dark Tide Rising – Deep Black Sea II (Permuted Press)
Forever Hunger

Made in the USA
Columbia, SC
06 February 2018